"HEY! WATCH OUT!
You Think You Own
This Place?"

"Cut it, Partini," Jerry said as he got to his feet.

"Well, who does he think he is?" Partini went on in the same loud voice.

"Partini!" Jerry threatened.

But, his black helmet still on, the cyclist had already turned, looking like a huge metallic insect, and stared at Jerry. Then his black helmet eye scanned each one of them as if he were checking every face, every button, every shoelace. Finally, he gave Jerry a last look, turned back, jumped on his kickstand, with his thick black cowboy boot, and walked slowly into the store. The screen door slammed behind him.

"Let's get out of here," Jerry whispered. Something in his gut was telling him to go.

MORELLI'S GAME

PATRICIA LEE GAUCH

AN ARCHWAY PAPERBACK
Published by POCKET BOOKS • NEW YORK

My special thanks to Ronald Gauch, Ed Martin, Addie Cetrulo and the C & O Canal Historical Society for their assistance.

An Archway Paperback published by
POCKET BOOKS, a Simon & Schuster division of
GULF & WESTERN CORPORATION
1230 Avenue of the Americas, New York, N.Y. 10020

Copyright © 1981 by Patricia Lee Gauch

Published by arrangement with G. P. Putnam's Sons
Library of Congress Catalog Card Number: 81-13880

ISBN: 0-671-45803-5

First Archway Paperback printing November, 1982

10 9 8 7 6 5 4 3 2 1

Printed in the U.S.A.

IL 7+

For Gerald Cetrulo, a wizard

MORELLI'S GAME

It Begins

"What's two hundred miles?" He looked like the hobbit he talked so much about, furry face and square body, pacing in front of the bikes in his hunched way. But a tall athletic hobbit. As he made a point, he sliced the air with his right palm, stopping abruptly at some invisible barrier, then he turned briefly to face the nine bodies in front of him.

"And you can look at those miles any way you want. I didn't tell you what to bring, and I'm not going to tell you how to get there." Turning away from them, he stretched over to a log and pulled himself onto it to study a spider that crawled across the bark. Then he squatted and looked up at the faces around him.

"Just don't call it a race. It doesn't have to do with speed. Got that? Sebastian, Bell . . . Templeton, you got that? It has to do with dragons and caves and green slime and Mirkwood . . ."

A tall black boy shrugged and looked aside as if to

say, not that crap again, and the man caught him. "*All right, Simpson, all right. Put it this way. You're wanderers . . . yeh, that's it. Wanderers. On a kind of journey. Okay? The only difference between you and most heroes is that you know you're starting from Fayette, Pennsylvania, you've got a map and five bucks.*"

One of the bikers, a blond in a Lockewood Academy shirt and a blue helmet, let his bike coast forward. "*Mr. Morelli, let me run through it. There are two teams. Each team is going to meet at the hostelry in Washington, D.C. Each team has five dollars, only five—no private funds allowed—and to get to Washington each team picks the way it wants to go: country roads, mountain roads, highways or whatever. And it's no race . . . but each team would like to get there first.*"

"*You got it, Templeton.*" The hobbit grinned.

A tall redhead tilted his head at him. "*How about an extra map . . . or two.*"

The man thought a minute. "*Yeh, yeh, that seems okay.*" He looked around again and hearing no questions, stood up.

"*What's the reward?*" a curly-haired boy with a bored look asked.

"*The reward, Partini! It's getting there, for God's sake!*" He hesitated for a moment. "*No, it's more than that.*" He looked up. "*That's where the ring is . . . yeh, Partini, that's it. The reward is a ring.*"

Jerry Sebastian looked down at his shoes. He heard Templeton mutter, "*A two-hundred-mile bike ride for a ring. Shit.*"

1

At first it sounded like a whirr behind Jerry, something
that spun a long way off, but he couldn't look. He was
too intent on the white lines that streaked under him.
Probably a small car back there, a Triumph, a BMW,
some arrogant foreign job trying to spook him. Unless
the creep couldn't see his flag?

But the noise didn't go away. Jerry regripped the
bars, trying to squeeze away the sweat between his
fingers, and that damned whirr, something bigger than
the thin whirr of his own bike. The road sloped into a
saucer turn and he pedaled harder and leaned into the
curve at a ridiculous angle. The noise followed him. It
was as if the thing were chasing him.

At the outer edge of the curve, he had to look back.
There were four blue helmets on bikes, the other team,
thirty maybe forty feet behind him. Where the hell had
they come from, barreling at him as if he were the lead

3

horse in the Kentucky Derby. Hadn't they heard: no race.

He glanced over his shoulder again. Bull Templeton was moving up, thick shoulders, thick chest, all that football blubber powering the bike toward him. Jerry clenched his teeth as he flattened himself to the bars.

"Move over, Sebast-head!"

Jerry could feel the muscles in his neck harden into steel cords. His legs moved like machines, pistons. He could feel the shadow of Templeton's white Fuji on his left when suddenly its front wheel dipped toward his rear wheel. He steadied his grip. The other bike swerved again.

"Hey, Sebast-head!" Bull hollered again, laughing.

Instinctively, Jerry jerked to the right and his front wheel careened into the soft gravel shoulder. Before the wheel could get rutted, Jerry jump-lifted it to the left and wobbled back onto the road. But his juices were churning now, and as the Fuji started to spin by, Jerry started a weaving pattern in front of the other bicycle.

Bull pulled up. Jerry kept his head down, his eyes on the weaving road.

"Sebastian!" Again. Let him bellow until he turned blue.

But his voice suddenly changed. "Heads up, Sebastian!"

Jerry looked up. Twenty feet ahead he saw a yawning black mouth that seemed to swallow the road. A tunnel. Jerry hunched over again, staring into the hole as he rode into it. Faint yellow lights clung to the tube walls and Jerry squinted as the coolness began vaporizing on his glasses. It was like looking through a fogged windshield. The white lights of oncoming cars raced at him like attacking eyes. A car whooshed at him from the rear, suddenly pulling him off balance.

Grinning, Bull pedaled by in the vacuum. Then as another car honked in back of Jerry, the other three shadows squeezed in front of him just before a blue Plymouth whizzed by the other way. No race, eh, Morelli, Jerry thought. Crap. Or to quote Bull himself, shit.

2

Jerry was determined not to blow. He bent his head under the metal spigot which sprouted miraculously out of a piece of concrete in the middle of the campground and splashed water on his mane of brown curly hair. Give the team thing a chance, his mother had said the day he had come home with the news of the trip and who was on his team. Give it a chance. "But don't expect too much from a private school," his newspaper-reporter father had said under his breath. Jerry hated to take sides. At Lockewood Academy only since September, he wasn't sure himself what he thought of it, except sometimes it seemed to give him the space he missed since leaving Vermont three years ago. But now, here he was in the middle of a no-race race with no sign of his team at the first stop. Unless you could count Thad Whiteford.

Suddenly, a stream of the icy spring water found its way down his chest to his belly, and Jerry turned his head over to catch the icy gush in his mouth, turning the image of Thad Whiteford at the picnic table upside down. Thad was trying to spread out three rolled maps at once, but each time he unrolled one, one of the others rolled back up. Tall, maybe six feet three, he had a long chin and a thatch of red hair that almost looked like a frazzled but pointed cap. Morelli always called him the wizard in class.

That, of course, was a laugh. Jerry shook out his wet mane and sat on the edge of the bench next to Thad who had finally managed to hold down the two maps by putting a cup of water on one edge and his bony thumb on the other, while he reached down with his free hand to the side of the bench for a rock to use as a weight. Naturally, the perfect rock lay just out of his reach. And naturally, as he reached the extra inch his thumb slipped off the map, the map rolled back up again, and turning, he lost his balance and fell backwards off the bench. Some wizard.

"Sorry," he said. Jerry reached over to help put him back together again. What Jerry's father had said for the fifty-fifth time that night was: private schools get the rejects of society. What can you expect from any team made up of private school kids? And his mother had said for the one-hundred-and-fiftieth time: "That is public school mentality, Charlie. Absurd. Children who are given enough room to grow can become individualists. Like a dogwood tree, Charlie, their branches spread and they blossom."

Discouraged, Jerry blew out a gasp of air and stood up to check the road. Bull and his team had whooshed by Madden Gap Park an hour ago. Of all people, Bull. When Jerry ran track no one could touch him, he was all streak, but somehow on the football field Bull got to him. And now this. It was no race; it was a rout! God, Jerry hated traveling in packs. Private school or public school, bag it all. Just give him a Vermont mountain and some free time on his own. That was living. Not this.

Redfaced but not in the slightest deterred, Thad leaned over almost secretively toward Jerry. "As I see it," he said, "we have to figure out Morelli's game."

In four weeks with their teacher Morelli, Jerry could brag that he hadn't had to say a single word to anyone in the class except Morelli himself, and those in one-word answers, but now clearly he was trapped.

"Yeh?" he managed to mumble.

"I mean," Thad went on, "we have to be on guard." Jerry nodded. "Morelli would never send us off on a cinch trip."

Jerry knew the hero's journey routine was coming because Morelli only had one routine. An English teacher who also coached football, if he started with Shakespeare, he ended with Tolkien and the hero's journey. If he started with an assigned poem by William Blake, he ended with Tolkien and the hero's journey. If there were a break in the locker room with five minutes to game time, it ended with Tolkien and the hero's journey: Someday, sometime when least expected, every person would get a call to go on a hero's journey. Tolkien had addled Morelli's brain.

"Dragons," Thad went on in that deep radio-announcer voice of his that didn't go at all with his grinning, freckled face. "We have to watch out for dragons, maybe a witch . . . an enchantress. A cave, there is always a cave to get through . . ."

Jerry looked around for an escape, but it was a miniature campground: two initialed tables and a plastic-lined garbage can.

"And The Threshold! I nearly forgot The Threshold." Thad sprang up, caught the button of his coat on a split edge **an**d recoiled into his cup of water, which spilt over his maps. As Thad reached for the cup, Jerry caught the maps before they rolled up again. "If we can figure out what The Threshold is, we can be on guard." A threshold was the spot where the hero fell into the risky part of his journey, and dragons tended to hang around thresholds. Quoth the Great Morelli. Sopping up the water, Thad went on as if nothing had happened while Jerry shook water off his hand and quickly walked over to the clearing. It was something of a disaster just being in Thad Whiteford's immediate area.

Where were the other guys anyway? Jerry walked farther down the sandy road toward the highway, but Thad's voice merely grew louder. "And of course we have to check our provisions, tire repair kit, our . . ." It occurred to Jerry that there was one consolation: the other team had gotten Peter Warren, the wizard's other half. As fat as Thad was thin, Peter Warren had to be a drag on any team. Morelli called him Gollum after Tolkien's whiney toad.

But it was a consolation short-lived as Jerry caught sight of two bicycle specks struggling up the slight hill into camp. Dave Partini came panting in first, wearing an orange headband with a matching orange sleeping bag and pack paniers stacked on the back of his slick new Peugeot bike. Chris Bell clanked up behind him, his pot-bellied mandolin-guitar and battered cowboy hat strapped over his back.

Jerry checked the sun, hanging low like a red balloon over the fringe of pine trees. There might just be time to get another hour of cycling in. Yes. But as Jerry started over to meet him, Partini started a barrage.

"I have had a dyspeptic back tire!" he announced as he climbed off his bike. "And where was the team?" He spun around in a circle on one toe, looking first at Jerry, then Thad. "I mean, I had to stand out in a ninety-five-degree sun and nurse a wheezing, flatulent tire alone. The smell of baking rubber was unbearable."

Jerry stopped in mid-step and half-grinned. You had to be careful with Partini and his twenty-round machine-gun mouth. Partini was a clown maybe, a comedian even, but you never knew who that mouth would hit.

"Well, where are we eating dinner?" he asked.

Jerry turned to Thad. There was light enough to cycle on: Wizard, say it!

But Thad turned to his maps. "See, I've got great maps, Partini." As he struggled across the campground with the rolls in his arms, one slipped out to the ground. Reaching for it, another slipped.

Disgusted, Partini turned aside. "All right, all right, I'll find my own place to eat." He impatiently propped his bike, a slick Peugeot PX10, against the tree. In his flowered orange headband around tight black curls, chinos which puckered at his pear-shaped waist, and Frye boots, he had a confidence that made Jerry feel almost undressed in his jean cutoffs and Lockewood tee shirt.

But right now all Jerry cared about was getting out of there. He passed over Partini to Chris Bell who had just come in and dropped his bike against a branch pile. There were no paniers at all on his bike, just a tired brown sack roped to the rear of an old riding seat; on the front, a kid's rusted horn barely clung to the handlebars. Bike, Chris, and sack looked like one dusty brown rumpled package that faded easily into the dark forest.

Jerry didn't care where he got his support. He just wanted to move on. He stared over the table toward Chris hoping that he'd see what they had to do. See that they could still move on. But Thad didn't give Chris a chance to see it.

Thad walked over to Chris, then to Partini, as if he were collecting an audience. "You see, we have to get inside Morelli's head. Know his game, I mean. He warned us about dragons and green slime . . . and . . ."

Partini shuddered at the word and belched. "Please, Wizard, not now."

"Sorry," Thad said.

Partini turned his head aside and, ignoring Thad, patted out a plush bed of needles, then, whistling, drew his sleeping bag neatly across them. Content with that, he carefully unfastened his paniers, slipped out a small, round mirror and tacked it onto a tree, briefly checking his teeth and chin. Then he pulled a bag of potato chips, a thermos jug, a long loaf of hard-crusted deli bread and giant jar of Smuckers peanut butter out of the paniers. Setting the items in an orderly line on the table, he took out a cloth napkin, drew it across his knees, and —slowly—started to cover a slice of bread with an inch of peanut butter. Partini was off the wall.

"But, your paniers are flat," Thad mumbled in disbelief. "Is that five days' food?"

"Hmmmmmmmm," Partini rumbled in a threatening hum. "I said, not now."

Jerry had a sudden urge to get some air, but Thad spit out quickly, "Where are your tire patches?"

Partini stopped and glared at him. "Wizard. Later. I am famished and you are bothering me. Just looking at your zitty face gives me severe gastric indigestion." He belched.

Zap.

Thad muttered something to himself.

"Wizard," Partini threatened, "shut up."

For a moment Thad sat back and tried to get Chris's eye, but Chris, having thrown his sleeping bag in a heap on a corner of the campsite, seemed to be going somewhere. Jerry stood up as if he were going somewhere, too. He really didn't know where. So Thad looked back at Partini, and words just burst out: "Well, if we don't have some kind of plan, we're just going to wander right into Mirkwood. We won't know which dragon hit us." His voice grew louder and louder.

"All right, all right." Partini picked up his napkin and threw it across the table. "I give up. You want someone to talk? Jerry's not good enough. Chris Bell is not good enough. OK. I'll talk. This is not a fairy tale, Wizard. You see that? It's not a game either, something you figure out, something you can plot." Thad sat back, his legs buckled together at the knees. "Because life's not that way," Partini went on. "Get it? You think because Bell has a mandolin, he's a bard? You think you're a wizard because Morelli said so? Take a good look. We're pathetic. We don't even have a hero."

Thad swallowed. "But you . . ."

"Me? I'm in some kind of race to Washington and I just learned to shift a ten-speed bike. Get the picture? Okay. Now, can I eat?"

Thad drew back and stared at the ground between his feet. "Sorry," he murmured.

"All right, look, I'll take care of the five dollars. Teamwork. See, now at least we're a team." Partini licked his fingers, then looked across at Jerry. "I smell something. Sebastian, I think it's your sneakers."

"Look, Partini—" Jerry started, his face flaming. He was quiet, not stupid. But Partini bent back over his potato chip sack, reached in and crumpled a handful of chips on his peanut butter sandwich.

Before Jerry could deal with him Chris touched Jerry's arm and nodded his head in the direction of a small path. Jerry felt the hairs on his neck bristle but he threw his paniers into his sleeping bag. When he turned around, Chris had gone. Humming, he had slung the mandolin, his strange eight-string brown bowl of an instrument, over his shoulder and loped onto a narrow, one-person path that seemed to lead away from the campsite downhill. Jerry could see Chris's head bobbing up and down above the long waffle grass as he descended the steep track.

Still angry, Jerry stalked after him down the incline toward a stream that grew louder as he approached. When the ground leveled off in a viney woods, he could see the dark stream ahead. Chris was already sitting on a rock, naked, with his dusty cowboy hat on, dangling his sneakers in the stream, strumming some weird melody and humming.

Jerry blew out a tired breath of air and reached into his pockets for raisins. Bull Templeton and those guys had probably pedaled their heads off to Maryland by now, and he had to be on this team. Breaking a small fanatic English class into two teams for some kind of mysterious trip was one thing, but stacking three first-string jocks and one crazy against three crazies and one jock didn't make sense.

Well, the day hadn't been a bust. He didn't know Morelli's game any better than Thad, but he wasn't going to stick around for this kind of circus. Dragons or no dragons, he knew he could get to Washington. He'd give the team thing one day. That was it. Then he'd move out alone.

3

Not certain if he ever did sleep, Jerry had gotten up first, thanks to a flock of squawking crows which had occupied every branch around the campsite for about fifteen noisy minutes and then flown away. He was glad Thad hadn't seemed to notice. They had enough to worry about without the wizard getting into the omen bit.

Besides, things were looking up. By nine o'clock Dave Partini had already taken his morning bath in the stream and come up smelling like he had raided a warehouse of Old Spice, Chris had retied his bundles on his bike with some kind of weird rope system, and Thad had polished his wrenches, laid out and repacked his screws, pliers, and inner tubes without falling over anything, and the team—such as it was—was off. They even stayed together, pedaling in a deep spiral out of Madden Gap toward the highway.

Thad led out, the red helmet that covered his thatch

bobbing ahead of Jerry. Anything but clumsy on a bike, those long legs knew what they were doing. And Jerry felt good, pedaling, pushing his pistons, hearing the whirr of his old but trim Peugeot. Not that anything had changed. He'd stick to them today, and if he took off tomorrow no one would be surprised. Jerry was a loner. They knew it at Trumbull High, and they already knew it at Lockewood. That bothered some people, but it didn't bother him. Alone when he ran track, alone when he biked home for lunch each day. Ever since they had moved to Pennsylvania three years ago his folks had even let him take his spring vacations alone in Vermont, not far from their old home. He was used to being alone.

Thad had spent so much time trying to figure out what Morelli's game was. Well, that could be the game as easily as any other: that the team would figure out there was one way to get to Washington fast, and that was for each person to go alone. But for today the plan was just to head south and make time. Alone or together, what they needed to do was to start. That was where Templeton was one up on them.

In a string they pedaled up a long, low hill past a *See Gettysburg* sign, then coasted down the other side, almost tire to tire, past a gray stone farmhouse, a barn skeleton. The morning sun was burning off a haze, and shrubs began to poke up through the ground clouds. It wasn't really clear what the country was like here, but Thad didn't let up for a minute. Even Partini was hanging in there. They were like a machine, barreling up and down the strange, low hills. Not bad, Jerry thought, not bad. Without thinking he started to look for Templeton's bike ahead.

Then, a half hour into the morning he saw Partini pedaling up beside him, his face a red mask of sweat.

"Stop at Sipe's Gap!" he shouted ahead to Thad. "I need air for my tire."

"I've got a pump," Jerry shouted back, the wind whipping his words away from him.

Partini pedaled frantically. "I need a station pump."

Jerry shook his head and hunched down lower, still on Thad's rear. But Partini kept it up. "And a bathroom!" Jerry might have known a hole in a leaf pile wouldn't do for Partini. Particularly when the choice of tissue was newspaper or nothing.

"That whole field is a bathroom!" Jerry shouted back again and motioned to his right.

"Yours maybe, Sebastian! Not mine!"

"All right, all right," Thad called back. It wasn't easy arguing at 25 miles an hour, and ten minutes down the road, he turned in a wide curve down the cutoff to Sipe's Gap.

Sipe's Gap turned out to be a grocery store that featured automobile equipment, pumped gas and looked as if it were sinking into an alfalfa field. A gas pumper–grocery clerk in faded overalls buckled across her chest stood at a ripped screen.

"I don't like it," Thad said as they coasted to the front of the building.

"What do you mean you don't like it?" Partini asked. He got off his bike, locked it, and taking his paniers over his arm, tucked in his pink button-down short-sleeved shirt with his free hand.

"Maybe it's her," Thad whispered, turning his back as the grocery clerk peered closer through the screen. "I think she's a witch."

17

Partini whispered at him through a smile, "Your mother wears combat boots," and walked toward the door swinging his paniers. Why he had to take them to the bathroom was beside the point.

Jerry and Chris fell in behind him, but the woman didn't budge when they approached the screen. That was all right with Jerry. He didn't want to be her best friend. He just wanted to use her john. Since he was there anyway, he wasn't going to pass up a toilet that flushed.

But she looked past Partini to Jerry and Chris. "We're closed," she said.

That was all right, too. He didn't want to buy anything. Jerry tried to peer around her shoulders for the Men's sign.

"Everything is closed," she finished, but she didn't take her eyes off the two of them.

Jerry shot a glance at Chris whose hair, past shoulder length, was pulled back into a neat pony tail, but whose kinky sideburns plumed out from his head. Self-consciously, Jerry pushed back his own neck-length curls. It was the hair; that's what bugged her.

Crazy woman. She had started to grab the inside door to close it when Jerry realized he really had to go. He looked around the side of the building for some handy bushes.

"Never thought of my hair as having a direct connection to toilets," Chris said under his breath. He had caught on too.

But suddenly, before she could draw the inner door shut, Partini leaned forward and sniffed toward the screen.

"I . . . smell . . . ginger root, don't I?"

18

She eyed him suspiciously. "Maybe."

"Hand ground. Yes, that's it, hand ground, and I smell real dill pickles . . . barreled in cider."

Her arms dropped slowly to her sides and she re-opened the door a crack. "Maybe."

"And . . . is it hand-ground cinnamon, too . . . or is it cinnamon . . ."

"Sticks," she helped, "from the East Indies."

"Now, there's a store!" Partini laughed. Bullshit in a button-down shirt. He had even adopted a country accent.

"I want to see that store, barrel by barrel . . . and the bathroom, ma'm," he said humbly. "Would you be so kind . . ."

But she hardened again and held on to the inside door. "Only if you'll get him off my rock."

At first Jerry thought she meant Chris, but there was no rock near them, and when he turned to discover one, she whispered, "He is one of yours, ain't he?"

Sitting on a huge, spreading piece of slate at the far side of the station, like a comfortable toad in a summer rock garden, was Peter Warren. His black hair hung in strings of sweat down his forehead and his two-day beard made him look ominous. A wet Lockewood Academy shirt struggled to cover his huge belly.

"No wonder the woman didn't want us to use her bathroom," Partini said. "Warren probably struck first."

Zap.

Peter waved, and gave them a big grin. "Your friendly traveling reject!" he called out.

"Peter!" Thad walked toward him, recovering quickly as he stubbed his sneaker on the bell hose that ran from the gas pumps to the store. The others followed.

19

Jerry cut to the side to avoid a ten-year-old jeep that skidded into the pump lane with a bushy-haired young man and a dirty-faced little kid in the front seat. It was a busy gas station for being parked in the middle of nowhere.

"I had wheel trouble late yesterday and this morning," Peter was saying, "and Bull and Simpson, well, they . . ."

The jeep honked.

"They waited for nearly an hour for me, but the screw kept loosening, I had no extra parts, the woman wouldn't let me use the phone here . . ."

"We know, we know," Chris muttered sympathetically. He took his mandolin from his shoulder and sat next to Peter. Across from them, the woman came smiling up to the gas pumps, nodding familiarly to the jeep, and wiped her hands on the bib of her overalls.

"I was hoping you'd come this way." Peter's several chins jiggled as he looked back and forth from Partini to Jerry to Chris to Thad to Partini again.

But Partini was watching the woman. "Look at that," he muttered. "She's almost friendly." A fume of gray smoke gunned out of the jeep's tail pipe as the woman shouted something to the young man from under the hood.

Thad started pacing in front of Peter. "It's fantastic, that's what it is. I mean, Pete's great on strategy." Thad turned to the others as if to beg support. "He knows maps, too. It'll be great."

"Wait a minute," Partini said, waving the fumes away and turning back with sudden interest. "What's great? That this Goodyear blimp catches up with his team?"

Thad blinked warily at Partini. "No. That Peter can come with us."

Partini turned on him. "Impossible! We'd never get in another bathroom in Pennsylvania . . . or Maryland."

A small spray of spit flew as Peter laughed, and Partini turned his back on him as if he had just uncovered a bowl of rotten eggs. "I smell armpits," he announced so loud the man in the jeep turned around.

Zap.

Jerry felt the anger working its way up through his neck again for the big blow. Ignoring it all, Chris had started to play an unrecognizable melody and midstrum had stopped and put his ear to the opening of the mandolin. "Only one gut string and it's going," he muttered. Thad sat next to Peter, dropping his arms between his knees. Partini was actually suggesting they leave Peter a hundred miles from nowhere. All this while Bull was widening his lead, and no one was going to say a damn thing.

"All right," Jerry said to himself as much as to anyone else. He had trouble enough getting words out, let alone when something bugged him. "What about the wheel now, the screw?"

"It's good now, Jerry, Chris. The screw's holding." Peter's lower lip swallowed his upper lip with pride and he patted an antique Raleigh hard-seater leaning on the rock next to him. But Partini had grabbed Jerry's sleeve and nodded at the woman and jeep driver heading away from the pumps.

"He's going into the store. She's softening," Partini said. "That's it. I'm going into the store too." But as he started across the pavement, a blast erupted behind him and a yellow Harley-Davidson motorcycle, chrome

21

back-rack and coiled-snake exhaust, wheeled onto the apron. Narrowly dipping in front of the rock, it spun within an inch of Jerry before it coasted to a stop at the pumps. Jerry jumped aside, catching himself against the rock.

"Hey!" Partini shouted. "Watch out! You think you own this place?"

"Cut it, Partini," Jerry said as he got to his feet.

"Well, who does he think he is?" Partini went on in the same loud voice.

"Partini!" Jerry threatened.

But, his black helmet still on, the cyclist had already turned, looking like a huge metallic insect, and stared at Jerry. Then his black helmet eye scanned each one of them as if he were checking every face, every button, every shoelace. Finally, he gave Jerry a last look, turned back, jumped on his kickstand, with his thick black cowboy boot, and walked slowly into the store. The screen door slammed behind him.

"Friendly country they've got here," Partini muttered picking up his paniers and brushing off some stones. Within the minute, Jerry saw the face of the woman press against the screen door, watching them. As he turned, two more cycles spun around the corner, narrowly missing Partini this time as they slid to a stop at the pumps.

"Locals!" Partini said as they climbed off their cycles —monster Kawasakis—and headed for the store.

"Let's get out of here," Jerry whispered. Something in his gut was telling him to go.

"With Peter?" Thad asked looking up under his thick white eyebrows at Jerry.

"With whomever." Jerry shrugged. The woman was

22

still watching them from the door. "Let's just get out of here."

Partini pushed his paniers back onto his arm and started across the station. "I'm not going until I get in that store. Everybody's invited but us? I have things to do . . . my bladder is . . ."

"I'm going." Jerry started in the opposite direction. Something in that store was on Partini's mind besides the bathroom but this was no time to figure it out. This place might be strange to them, but clearly they were the strangers to the woman and the cyclists.

"Come on," Partini pleaded to the others. "There are five of us, four, surely . . ."

But one after another the others filed after Jerry. Thad grinned broadly as he helped Peter to his feet. "I knew those crows meant something this morning. I just didn't know it was going to turn out good."

At the side of the store, they climbed on their bikes and stood looking at each other. "Well, do we go the eastern or the western route?" Thad finally asked. He was grappling for his maps.

"Clearly a question for the great strategist Gollum!" Partini bowed to Peter who looked around the circle of faces but said nothing. Another useless one, Jerry thought. Alone these guys would go down the tubes.

"All right," Jerry finally asked. The quicker they got out of there the better. "Which way did Templeton go?"

"East, yes, he went east out of the mountains," Peter said eagerly looking at Jerry with dark round eyes.

"Then, let's go west," Chris said quietly. Jerry hadn't even realized Chris was listening.

Thad had trapped one map across his handlebars. "That will be to Indian Pool," he said.

"Indian Pool then," Chris repeated and coasted away without waiting for any more discussion.

The five of them spun out of the driveway in a line. As Jerry looked back at the store, the screen door was empty.

"It's like another country," Thad said as he pedaled past the crumbling gas station sign.

"Yeh," Chris added. "Not ours."

Jerry realized he didn't have to go to the john anymore. He wasn't sure why.

4

When the five bikes swept onto the highway, Thad
dropped behind to keep Peter company as he struggled
red faced and panting up the first hill. Partini fell back,
too, and it left Jerry and Chris to ease out in front,
cutting the wind and a road which seemed to spin out
endlessly in front of them. "Thirty miles to Indian
Pool," a sign that needed to be repainted said. Not bad.
A stretch to pick up time against Bull. But for some
reason, from the moment he turned onto the highway
Jerry couldn't keep his mind on Bull Templeton or anything else. He felt more and more as if he were in a
strange country.

Huge gray boulders poked up out of the ground and
pushed the grass into narrow valleys. Even the scrubby
trees seemed to struggle for a piece of ground. The haze
was long gone, but the rocky fields looked deserted, the
stone farmhouses empty. Jerry heard Chris moving up
closer and closer, his roped-on packs and mandolin

clanking and his no-tune hum growing louder. Neither of them said anything, which wasn't surprising since Chris was as quiet as Jerry in class. The two of them just kept pace, their feet cycling in perfect tandem down the endless highway, but then Chris moved up alongside him.

"Think that gas station was The Threshold?" he shouted. Jerry could see him grinning as the wind tore his words away from him.

"What do you mean?" Jerry shouted back. He already knew.

"Morelli's game!" Chris shouted again. Shouting into the wind was like shouting into a wall.

"Where are the dragons?" Jerry got out, as a small red pickup rumbled by, forcing them back into single file. Every threshold had its dragons.

"That gas station wasn't exactly inhabited by friendly natives!" Chris shouted ahead.

A Volkswagen bug forced the two of them farther apart. Jerry didn't mind admitting it to himself: dragons were for the Morelli fans, but it didn't make him feel sad to get out of that gas station while the "friendly natives" were still in the store. In fact, the more distance they put between themselves and the store the better.

As the miles stretched out, he began to feel better about the strange rocky country they were riding through. Chris and he had pedaled farther and farther ahead of the others. Jerry liked the alone feeling he got biking out that way and, except for the occasional trucks that came roaring up on them like giant Tonka toys, the two whirred along the empty highway with no trouble. Chris was even trying to hum again over the wind—another weird no-tune—but it had a sort of hypnotic power about it. Jerry almost liked it.

In his mind he went over Bull's route and how they might cut him off or make up for lost time. Whatever the reason, Jerry's mind was a hundred miles away when he saw the bridge. It came into his view at the top of a hill that looked as if it fell off into nothing. But they had started to coast down before he spotted a motorcyclist in the shade under the bridge. Jerry shot a quick glance at Chris who had stopped humming and was staring at it, too.

A cold chill ran down Jerry's neck. It couldn't be one of the cyclists they had seen in the station. No cycles had passed them on the highway. Jerry ran through what had passed them: a Volkswagen, a pickup—no, two pickups—a green milk truck. But then, as the gray sweep of bridge grew larger in front of them, Jerry saw the cyclist, his shiny black helmet still on, lying against the back-rack of his motorcycle with his feet up, apparrently sleeping. Or waiting.

Jerry and Chris tightened their tandem. A fairly empty highway would naturally attract cyclists. All kinds. But as they pedaled closer into the shade of the bridge, the yellow metal belly of the cycle came into view, and Jerry caught sight of the black cowboy boots crossed casually over the handlebars.

Neither Jerry nor Chris spoke. The cyclist didn't move his black insect head an inch as the two of them started under the bridge, their double whirr suddenly louder. His arms stayed crossed around his studded black jacket. Jerry stared straight ahead as they biked within ten feet of him. His heart beat cold against the

27

inside of his shirt, but he stared ahead. The black figure didn't move.

In the light again, Jerry turned to Chris.

"It couldn't be the same guy!" Chris said.

"I know," Jerry said.

Ten minutes up the road, ten minutes of watching and listening, they approached a Holiday Inn billboard, its triangular shadow stretching across an empty field. Behind it they spotted three cycles: two black, one yellow. Black-visored insects, sleeping. Or watching. Or waiting. That was impossible, too. Jerry felt the perspiration dripping down onto the neck of his shirt as he pedaled past the billboard, the rim of Chris's front wheel nearly touching his. But again, nothing came roaring at their backs.

"How could they get ahead of us?" Chris said as soon as the billboard was out of sight. Jerry looked across the countryside, the low hills, the blank-looking farmhouses. There was something in those hills that they didn't know about, maybe a network of roads like webs.

At the top of every hill, they no longer expected the road to fall off and they waited for the familiar specks on a sprawling gray rock above the highway or lounging by a creek under an overpass. But for miles there was nothing. Suddenly, it came to Jerry.

"We're all right, Chris," he shouted out.

Chris rattled up alongside him.

"They're not going to do anything. Don't you see?" The cyclists knew that just expecting something to happen was enough.

Jerry broke his thought off when he saw the tiny deserted vegetable stand with its empty eyes and broken TOMATOES-FOR-SALE sign just down the highway. Automatically, Jerry searched the shadows. Then he caught himself. That's what the cyclists wanted. They wanted them to expect and expect. And expect! Jerry jammed his foot angrily onto the pedal. The dead building had just swept by as the roar blasted at them out of the opposite field. Jerry jerked his head around. Three cycles, led by the yellow one, bounced out across the field toward them and spun onto the highway. Three giant one-eyed insects.

God almighty! He and Chris weren't watching silent specks anymore.

Jerry tightened his grip and pedaled ahead, but the yellow cycle gunned its way in front of him howling, "YAAAAAAAAAAAAAAAAA!" It didn't seem human.

"What do you want?" Jerry shouted back.

But there was no answer as the other cycles pushed their way into the space between Chris and him, howling in return, "YAAAAAAAAAAAAAAAAAA!"

Jerry's neck throbbed wildly. "What do you want?" he shouted again, but the yellow cyclist had wound his motor down so slow that Jerry's front wheel started to wobble. He'd have to brake. Then suddenly the cycle gunned across the highway in a loop and pulled in behind Jerry's bike, lapping at his rear wheel. Jerry jumped on his pedal to pick up speed and started into a wide curve. No time to see what had happened to Chris.

"YAAAAAAAAAAAAAAAAAA," the voice behind him wailed again, as the cyclist gunned his motor. At least Bull Templeton had a face! Jerry gripped his bars and drove his sneakers into the pedals on the curve.

Suddenly from somewhere behind him, Chris shouted, "Heads up, Jerry!"

Jerry looked up to see a hay wagon turning slowly out onto the highway from a side road, a hundred feet ahead of him. "Hey!" Jerry burst out at it.

The hatless guy on the tractor never even looked at him. The wagon just loomed larger and closer. Frantically, Jerry squeezed his brakes, but he was cycling too fast. It threw him off balance. He could feel his weight swing, the frame wobble. Helplessly he careened across the center strip to the left, but the yellow cycle and the two black ones swept up from behind whipping around the nose of the tractor on a thread of pavement, forcing Jerry to steer wildly into the gravel shoulder. His sneakers flew out of the pedals as he tumbled through the air and landed on his side, his chin stinging in the sheet of stones. As he lay there, he could hear the motorcycles' whine fading down the highway.

It had started to rain when Partini, Thad and Peter rode by and Chris waved them on.

5

As he and Chris pedaled down the main street of Indian Pool a memory jabbed Jerry. Of Ed Anderson. Redheaded Ed Anderson. He had tracked Jerry like an angry shadow during Jerry's first days at the middle school when he was fresh from Vermont. Tracked him. Waited for him. Outside the locker room. Outside the school yard. Outside the pharmacy. Redheaded Ed Anderson, mean for no reason.

It was Ed Anderson all over again.

The soft rain had turned into a pelting spring storm, but after he and Chris pedaled the length of the town twice, they found the others crouching with a strange girl under a band shell in a park nearly as large as the town itself. That didn't make sense either, and Jerry suddenly grew furious at them for sitting there—just sitting there—dry and unconcerned as if nothing had happened. And with a girl. Great.

"Hey!" Chris said, smiling and walking lazily up to

the peeling, rain-slicked band shell. Incredible. He didn't seem to even notice the rain except that he had folded his mandolin under his sack and had cradled it between his shoulder and chin.

"Hey, hey," Partini replied. He was sitting next to a plumpish black-haired girl in a peasant skirt and blouse with a Taiwan daisy button. "Come meet Mimi. She's thirteen. Greek. Has brown eyes that dance and smells a helluva lot better than Gollum."

Peter grinned at Partini and dropped his chin into the folds of his neck in a supportive nod. Thad, next to him, had three rolled maps under his arms which he was trying to juggle as he looked for a dry spot in the middle of the band shell. Angry at the whole scene, Jerry peeled off his sneakers and socks and wrung them out.

"God! Those sneakers smell worse than the town dump after a ten-day heat wave," Partini whispered to Mimi.

Jerry deliberately ignored him and looked across at the few stores and buildings that lined the empty street. The rain poured harder, beating noisily on the wooden pavilion. Although it was only somewhere around six, it was already getting dark and heavy.

"Something bugging you, Great Jerry the Sebastian? Tell us," Partini mocked and nudged the girl cuddling next to him.

Chris looked quickly at Jerry. When he didn't answer, Chris nodded. "Yeh . . . ah . . . maybe," he began.

But Jerry broke in. "First, let's find somewhere to spend the night, someplace dry and nearby, okay?"

Partini edged forward still staring at Jerry.

But Mimi suddenly fluffed her skirt and climbed down. "Look, I know a place back of Main Street, a barn. The house is locked but the barn is empty, just used for storing hay. There may be leaky spots but . . ."

"How far?" Jerry asked. He couldn't take his eyes off the street.

"Five minutes," she said.

"Down the highway?"

"No, back roads."

"Is there a place to hide the bikes?"

"Behind the barn."

Jerry nodded, scooped his paniers over his arm. "You first. . . ."

Mimi looked up at Partini who shrugged with a slightly bored expression and grudgingly started to stand up. "What's wrong with him," he whispered to Chris.

"He met a dragon," Chris said.

6

There were still chickens in the barn, and as Mimi ran from the house's crumbling porch to the barn door and tried to pull it open, three came squawking out. Peter ran through the rain with some neighbor's discarded, yellowed newspaper over his head and, taking in a huge swallow of air, he pulled the door wide enough for the others to squeeze through the crack. As chickens scattered out, one flapped into a half-buried plow bit and Peter picked it up, stroking it while Jerry and the others squeezed into the barn.

"Chickens are ridiculous," Partini muttered as he looked past Peter clutching the bird to a room so dark only cracks of light broke through the splintered siding. "But then so are some people."

Jerry hardly heard him. He kept listening for sounds. It didn't make sense for him to listen. They were two blocks off the highway in a deserted barn, but he kept listening.

34

"Wait here," Mimi said. She felt her way along a shadow wall to a tiny doorway, pushed at a thick door and slid through. The sounds of her fingers feeling across the wall seemed louder in the dark as the five stood there waiting. Finally she squeezed back into their room with a dust-caked lantern which she had already lit.

"Not bad, eh?" she said perkily. Something about her was more assured than any thirteen-year-old Jerry had ever met. Certainly his sister or any of her friends. "We have parties in here." She grinned as the light spread across her face. "Good parties."

"But no one much knows about this barn?" Jerry asked.

"No one much." She grinned.

She wound the lantern's wick higher, sending a kerosene smell into the hay-damp air. Jerry found himself searching the corners. The barn was divided into two lofts with a center ground strip littered by a broken reaper and parts of machines which weren't even recognizable buried in loose hay. Only a pitchfork still clung to an otherwise empty row of nails. He could hear feet finding their way in the hay.

Chris sat down and started to tune his mandolin in a dark corner. Nothing seemed to faze him for long.

"Look . . ." Jerry began.

"Not here," Mimi said. "Too wet. Upstairs there's a loft."

Jerry impatiently climbed up a slatted wall ladder behind her to reach a loft stacked with bales of hay. Mimi hooked the lantern on a nail, and it flickered as storm winds found cracks through which to blow. Roof rain drained down a center pole into a pool of loose hay.

Peter squatted in one corner with his bike pack and sleeping bag clutched under his arm as if he were waiting, not for Jerry to talk, but for someone to tell him what to do. The chicken, a brown and white speckled hen, still shook quietly in the hay next to him.

Thad pulled out his plastic bags of food. "I am stupid," he chanted, "stupid. Everything I have has to be boiled in water!" He didn't look much like a wizard now with his red hair plastered around his head in dark streaks. He burrowed in his sack for something else, dumping packages and utensils everywhere as he searched and mumbled constantly. Next to him Chris pulled out a rag from his sack and started wiping his mandolin, humming softly.

It was as if Jerry were in the center of an amusement-park mixer ride that was turning faster and faster, but bits kept flying off.

"Well?" Partini started.

"Hmmmm?" Peter looked up. No one had told him what to do yet. Partini ignored him.

"Let's talk about dragons."

"Dragons?" Thad's hands slowly fell to his knees and his voice echoed in the cavernous barn.

"Haven't you heard?" Partini whispered in mock mystery. "Our Jerry caught one! Right, Jer?"

Jerry could feel his neck bristle. Partini went on, "Or did it catch you?"

Chris put his mandolin down, listened for a moment, then hearing no one speak began, "It's simple, we . . ."

But again Jerry picked up his own pieces. "That

Harley-Davidson we saw at the gas station almost buggered us today."

Partini stood up. "That's it? That's the dragon? You look fine to me. Now, do I get to tell you about the blisters on my tush? There's a real problem. I can hardly sit down . . ."

"There were three of them eventually," Chris added from his corner.

"What color were the cycles?" the girl asked. Jerry didn't know why she didn't go home. What about her parents anyway? Like the ad said: "Do you know where your children are?" But she didn't budge.

Jerry told the others. "It was just the yellow Harley-Davidson at first, then the two black Kawasakis rushed us."

At these words, Mimi sat back in the hay.

"Do you know them?" Thad asked. The lantern caught his shadow in a new light and threw it grotesquely up the wall.

"I'm not sure," she said.

Thad looked at her for a moment then turned to Jerry worriedly.

"What happened?" he asked.

"They ran us into a hay wagon."

Partini stood up and started to scuffle through the hay. "Come, come, come Sebastian. Why would the big bad motorcycles want to bugger two puny bicycles? Surely in your genius-sized brain you can see that doesn't make sense."

"It doesn't," Jerry answered. "That's just the trouble."

"Well," Partini interrupted, "so, all the more reason to have a party now. You're here and they're gone."

Chris started picking at his mandolin, but his eyes were following Jerry.

"Maybe," Jerry said. He was still listening.

"Let's not be dramatic, Sebastian. What do you mean 'maybe'? On roads there are going to be cars, trucks, motorcycles, big motorcycles, small motorcycles. Those aren't dragons, those are called machines."

"Wait," Jerry clipped off Partini's sentence. He did hear something, a faint sound of a motor, maybe more than one.

"It's a car, Sebastian," Partini said.

But no one moved. Peter's hands unclasped his pack. The sound was too high to be the whine of a car, too big to be a mower, too . . . Jerry felt suddenly relieved they had locked their bikes behind the barn. The sound slowed. Jerry stared at Peter's thick toad shadow against the wall. Another motor joined the first and they buzzed slowly along the street.

"Are you all crazy?" Partini said. "What do you think, we're being followed or something?"

No one answered, and, finally, the buzz moved down the street. Peter took a tomato out of his pack—permission or no permission—and stared anxiously from face to face.

"I'll get the maps," Thad said, scrambling through the hay toward the ladder. "I mean, there are small, hairline roads we could bike. Something unknown. I mean, what we need is a plan." He muttered all the way to the ladder.

"Wizard," Partini hissed, brushing off dirt that had fallen from the beams, "take your plan and your maps, shove them in a carcass-filled cesspool and jump in. I'm getting out of here. This barn smells like fried sneakers and the outhouse of a two-hundred-cow barn. Disgusting." He had his paniers with him again.

"Partini." Jerry clenched his fist in the hay.

"Look," Mimi had started over to the ladder but turned around, "I don't know about maps and plans, but . . ." Something about her putting in her two cents where she didn't belong really got to Jerry. ". . . sometimes cycles around here guard their turf, but, well, there is a way to get away from them. You could get off the highways altogether by riding the towpath."

Thad muttered down the ladder, hay shaking down around him as he climbed. "My maps have everything: notes, trails, mileage . . ."

"Stow it, garbage," Partini said.

Peter bit into the tomato, the seeds dribbling down his chin as he listened. Partini looked away with disgust. "Go on, Mimi," he said.

"It's just a few minutes from here. It's the path the mules walked along to pull barges on the canal fifty years ago. A path right next to the canal. It was a wild, fighting trail back then, but, well, time sort of left it behind."

Peter stopped chewing and looked up. The pupils of his eyes seemed huge.

"It's narrow and . . ."

"Shhh," Jerry interrupted. His ears were as sensitive to sounds as a German shepherd's. The tinny motors again, somewhere nearer. They sounded as if they were cruising directly in the street in front. A hesitation. Then a single motor turned down the driveway to the house. Jerry soundlessly clutched the hay. The sound, a continuous buzz grew closer, stopping somewhere near the rear of the house. For seconds. A minute. Then in a burst, the buzz started again and seemed to circle the rear of the house slowly. Finally it faded back down the street.

Jerry felt a boot in his gut. He turned quickly to Mimi.

"The towpath," he prodded.

"No stop lights, flat. It goes directly to Washington."

"Express!" Partini added.

Mimi nodded. "Sometimes with all the trees around it, it almost looks like a tunnel."

"A tunnel," Jerry repeated. He thought about the last tunnel he had been in. "What about the motorcycles?"

"No motors allowed."

"Can anyone get to it from the highways?" Jerry asked. He didn't much want Bull Templeton and those creeps on it either.

"The next direct access from the highway is at Brunswick, but that would be a backtrack. Someone would have to know about the towpath to cut in there to pick it up." It was almost as if she knew what he was thinking. "And cops patrol the junctions . . ."

"What are the drawbacks?" Jerry asked. There had to be some.

The girl sat down, pulled her skirt over her knees and sat back against the post. "I don't know. I guess storms can mess up the towpath, but a good cyclist can get past that. The hurricane messed it up bad last year, a lot of washouts, but the ones around here have been fixed . . . and a railroad runs along the canal, sometimes you see a few creeps who ride the rails, but . . . no, I can't think of any other drawbacks."

With a flourish of his jacket flap, Partini walked over

to the ladder. "Enough, enough. Sounds good to me. Even old Morelli didn't figure we'd find an express tunnel to Washington. Meanwhile, I'm getting out of here for some pure air."

"With those sounds out there?" Thad asked, still looped over the ladder.

"With this smell and Gollum eating a tomato in that disgusting way, I have no choice. Besides I need water." He grabbed his paniers.

"Partini, I have water," Jerry said. Something about Partini's having to get away again didn't sit right.

"Look, Sebastian, don't try to be a hero. I'm getting my own water. Mimi, coming?"

"Not now." She smiled and looked across at Jerry, but he ignored her.

"You're crazy going out with those motors patrolling the streets," Jerry said.

"Then, my dear and Great Sebastian, I'm crazy." He pushed past Thad and climbed down out of the loft. "Besides," he called out at the top of his lungs as he shuffled through the hay corridor below, "if I'm going into an express tunnel, I need one more hour of freedom."

Jerry settled back, the sharp edges of the hay prickling him, and listened as Partini pushed open the door. But all he heard was the sound of the rain which had started to pick up and noisily pelt the tin barn roof. Nothing else.

"There is one thing," Mimi whispered as the rain started to drain noisily down the pole. "Could I come?"

7

The girl had been right. Next morning the towpath spun out in front of them through a dark, leafy archway that reminded Jerry of the tunnel where he had raced Bull. But this one arched over the path and the canal that ran alongside it, and it seemed endless. So did the trees and fields that stretched out on either side. No cars, no trucks, no yellow sounds. Not that Jerry was going to stop listening until they got to Washington. Maybe he'd never stop listening.

Jerry looked ahead to a tree stump whose roots spread like fingers across the towpath, jumped his bike over them and pedaled on. Thad had refused to start out first, mumbling something about a hunch he had had in the middle of the night. More likely he was pouting over their accepting Mimi's idea. And Partini's mood had gone from dramatic to impossible when the others agreed: no Mimi on the trip. (What would Morelli say if they showed up in Washington with a thirteen-year-old kid?) But even Partini had agreed they should make Sharpsburg today: forty-five miles, and now they were spinning out with no problems, as if they had been cast in a single line down the tunnel. Not only were they escaping the dragons, it was exactly the kind of cut-off Jerry had hoped they'd discover to pick up time on Templeton.

Jerry heard clanking moving up close behind him. He was learning to expect it.

"Do you think Morelli figured this tunnel?" Chris called ahead to him.

"No," Jerry shouted back over his shoulder. "It's too easy. I think Morelli figured we had all gotten a little soft in our private-school world. He figured we'd fumble around those mountain roads." Jerry realized he was feeding in a little bit of his father's "public-school mentality," but it did strike him he was saying "we" not "you."

"Then maybe we've put one over on Morelli," Chris said after another long pause.

"Maybe," Jerry shouted back.

Fields followed fields, none the same. A field of blue flowers, maybe bluebells, waved like a morning sea to the edge of a rail fence. A golden field sloped down to the dark wood, and violets backed up against the towpath slope. The five bicyclers swept by them all, passing the concrete canal locks every five miles or so. The locks had been used to raise or lower the water for the barges, but now they were closed or broken, just handy to tick off time: Lock 49, Lock 48, Lock 47. Zero lock would be Washington.

"Is there a town coming up?" Partini shouted ahead so even Jerry heard it four bikes up.

"No!" more than one of them called back.

At the Conococheague Aqueduct, they all walked their bikes across the stretch of concrete that used to funnel the canal water across the brown muddy river below—water across water—and Partini hustled into the center of the pack.

"There has to be a town ahead," he said.

Jerry tried to look back at him. What was on Partini's mind this time? Air for his tire? Water? Bathroom? They were beginning to sound a lot like excuses. But Jerry soon forgot Partini.

The aqueduct was incredible. Barges used to float where he was walking—right over the river. And mules used to walk here. He could almost hear hooves on the boards, but there was no stopping. At the other side, they coasted off into the tunnel again, and in moments they were all pedaling—Peter, the sweat running down his back sketching dark shadows on his shirt, Chris, his pack smacking noisily as he hit tree roots—all of them except Partini who shouted, "If we don't stop soon I'm going to be nauseous!" His voice jerked as his bike whacked against a bridge of roots. "At a town!" he added.

Then when they had been out on the trail an hour, a town appeared out of nowhere. They turned a corner and across the railroad tracks that ran close to the path at this point, some roofs pinnacled across the field. A tiny wooden canal house sat at the lock nearby as if it were the gate house to the city. Purple violets spread down from the house and into the soft clipped grass.

"Hurray for civilization," Partini yelled. "Telephone booths, concrete streets, cars!" Jerry looked back to see

44

Partini slowing his bike into the gate-house path. "Whoop!"

But Thad's head was stubbornly bent, and as Partini and Chris and Jerry pulled up, Thad bicycled right past them. He never looked up, and without any discussion Peter followed him.

"Hey, Gollum! Wizard! Freaks!" Partini shrieked as they pedaled ahead, but they didn't turn around, and Partini's machine-gun mouth couldn't take aim. Jerry wanted to laugh out loud. Whatever it was Partini was up to was hitting hard times. Jerry and Chris climbed back on their bikes and followed Thad and Peter.

"Ridiculous!" Partini shouted.

"They're the bosses," Jerry shouted back.

But later, three or four miles into the path, when they stopped at Lock 43 and pulled their bikes up over to the side, Partini was nowhere in sight.

At first Jerry didn't think anything about it. Peter collapsed like a mountain on the bridge, not even avoiding the hot afternoon sun, a sweaty band of stomach sticking out from under his shirt. Thad struggled to balance his bike against his knee to get his food out. When the wheel swung away, the unsnapped panier fell upside down and dumped the wrenches. What a team.

Jerry felt the heat flow up around his neck and eyes as he stretched out. The insides of his legs ached; that one spot, where the seat had rubbed against his thigh, was raw. His fourth finger was blistered, rubbed raw from a ragged edge of his taped handlebars. The mountain next to him panted. And sweated. Poor Gollum. At Jerry's feet Chris, smiling but ignoring them all, shuffled over to the edge of the canal. Musty with lily pads that floated around fallen logs, the canal was brown and gummy but peaceful. Jerry realized he had stopped listening for at least half an hour. Chris started humming. Just once Jerry wanted to recognize a tune.

After twenty minutes, Partini still hadn't come, and all three of them seemed to be looking at Jerry.

"Well, Jer," Thad said.

"Well what?" Jerry answered.

"What should we do about Partini?"

Even Chris watched him.

"What do you want to do?" He knew how to hand a ball back as well as the next person.

"Wait," said Peter.

"Go on," said Thad.

Partini was right. They really were looking for a hero, one hero to give them answers, answers. Just because he had said a few words the night before they figured he was it. Wrong. The only reason he hadn't cut out last night was survival. That sure as hell didn't make him a hero.

But as he looked up, he noticed the towpath growing darker. The sun had ducked under a shelf of low clouds.

"May as well go. Partini can't get lost in the tunnel," Jerry said, and he flipped his leg over the bar and coasted into a start.

The minute they rode off Jerry knew they were in trouble. Giant clouds had gathered again, and within half an hour the trees ahead of them turned silver as a brisker and brisker wind twisted its way into the tunnel, throwing itself like a wall against the bikes. The four of them jammed close together as Jerry kept the lead and bent into the wind.

"My mandolin!" Chris shouted, but Jerry kept pushing ahead. Sharpsburg had to be only ten miles up the path.

"Maybe we'd better stop," the wizard called out.

Jerry ignored both of them. There was nowhere to stop. On his right a granite bank sloped out from the towpath toward the Potomac. No overnight spots there. No canal houses to hide behind. Just fields bent flat from the wind, and branches tossing like arms in a wild dance. Each turn of the pedals took a hard push. He just hoped Partini could handle this alone.

But then Peter wailed from the rear, "Jerry!"

"There's no place," Jerry shouted back. What a mess.

"Play a hunch then," Thad called ahead.

"I haven't got any." Jerry could feel his voice being torn from him by the wind.

But after another mile, just past Lock 40, Thad called again. "Jerry!"

By now Jerry struggled just to remain upright, but when he turned this time, he saw the three of them had stopped riding. Thad and Peter had pulled their bikes over on their sides and were running, paniers in their arms, toward the Potomac River. Chris, huddled in the middle of the towpath over his mandolin, was trying to pull his bike off to the side. Crazy fools. Jerry turned around as large drops of rain started pelting his back. Sharpsburg, where are you! Partini, where are *you!*

He gave one quick glance down the path. Nothing. Then, he ran his bicycle back until he reached the trail in the woods the others had run down.

"Chris?" he called over the shushing leaves.

"Go ahead," Chris shouted. They were only five feet away from each other, but the wind was so loud, their voices got lost. Still struggling with his falling bundles, bike and mandolin, Chris motioned Jerry on.

Midway down the trail, Jerry turned. "Leave something in the path for Partini!" Then he turned back again and shouted, "Gollum! Where are you going . . ." but he realized the other two had disappeared. Rain trickled down his neck, the wind tore his bike out of his hands at every step. Ahead of him he could hear the Potomac itself turning into a cauldron of waves. He could feel the pieces flying away from him again. This was no place to stop!

8

At first Jerry's ears picked up nothing he recognized.
Then over the wind ripping through the grove of trees,
he heard a cry, "Here!" Jerry started running toward
the sound, letting his bike jar across the wet rocks, until
he stopped at a ledge facing the river. "Here!" a voice
said again faintly. It seemed as if the sound were coming from above him because there was nothing around
him. Then he saw a dark patch in the ledge as it layered
into a small hill. A low but wide-mouthed cave fringed
with sodden moss dug its way under the bank.

Jerry pushed his bike under some thick bushes and
crawled carefully over to the slippery entrance, the last
ten feet on his hands and knees across the rain-slicked
rock. He had never seen a cave in Vermont, though
caves must be there, full of rocks and underground
rivers. As he ducked inside, he shuddered.

Peter sat like a tremendous Gollum-toad against the
wall, pointing a small penlight into the deepest part of

the cave where the feeble arc of light fell off into a dark hole. Thad's hair stood out in back of him, shadowed against a gray limestone wall and the deep black mouth.

"Thad had a hunch," Peter whispered, ". . . at least it's dry."

The cave might be out of the storm, but it was damp as rain. Jerry shuddered again when Chris came up behind him on his Indian feet.

"Whew . . ." he whistled, stepping into the cave opening in front of Jerry and shaking his mandolin.

"What do you mean a hunch, Thad?" Jerry asked and looked around. "You don't expect me to believe, you just happened . . ."

"There's more back there." Thad's words echoed deeply. He seemed to enjoy the sound of his own voice in the hollow room. "More," he said, roundly echoing, and he started over a rock that humped into a black hole. "If we crawl back . . ."

"Wizard," Jerry warned. "Wait a minute." He tried to say it calmly, knowing how easily Thad was unfooted, but Thad was bending back farther and farther into the cave, swinging his head from side to side to avoid the low ceiling hung with jagged edges of dripping moisture.

The wind whistled outside, squeezing between loose stones at the entrance, sending an eerie moan into the cave. Thad's light fell off into nothing Jerry could see. "Don't be stupid, Thad." Thad inched forward. "Stop! Whiteford, you don't know what . . ." but suddenly Thad's elbow brushed up against a rock finger that snagged his jacket. It pulled him around, and his left foot slipped down the far side of the hump. Thad's light beam slid across the ceiling as he fell into the darkness on the other side.

"Thad!" Jerry grabbed Peter's flashlight and crawled toward the other beam on his stomach. No chances now. "Thad!"

As the light beam steadied on the ceiling, a faraway voice said, "Here."

Jerry inched his way across the cold, wet hump of rock, the slime rubbing off on his shirt and stomach as he pulled himself to the edge. There, where a thin ledge protruded around the far side, Jerry pointed the light down into the crevice. Eight feet, nine feet below, Thad, his knees bent, one arm extended up a hulky cracked stone, lay in a twisted heap not unlike one of the rock heaps next to him.

He stuck his arm up. Chris had crawled alongside Jerry, and the two of them stared down into the hole.

"Sorry," Thad said.

Jerry stretched down the hump, extending his arm toward Thad's free one. Their hands did not touch. "Anything feel broken or hurt?" Jerry muttered.

"No, just bent," Thad said. He pushed himself around, untangling his legs from the rocks at the bottom. His beam of light flew around the ceiling as he struggled to get his footing, then he reached again.

Chris crawled back and sat on Jerry's legs as Jerry stretched farther and farther down the hump. When he finally touched Thad's fingertips, Jerry was hanging over half-way down the slippery hump himself. He pulled himself another six inches forward to get an Indian grip, then he started to move back but Chris was still fastened to his legs.

"Let up," Jerry said.

He inched back slowly, but as Thad braced his feet and pulled, Jerry started to slide forward across the edge.

"Bell!" he shouted, and again Chris threw himself across his legs. Jerry laid his face on the rock a minute, then tried once more.

"Can I help?" Peter said, crawling onto the hump with the two of them, but he just squeezed them against the wall.

"Not now, Gollum!" Jerry grunted, "Not now." Thad had flattened his stomach against the rock and had begun to wedge his knee against it to pull himself up. Jerry inched back slowly, slowly.

"Grab his other arm, Chris," he yelled, and Chris unloosed Jerry's legs and crept forward across the slimy rock to grasp Thad's other arm. As they both pulled, in inches, Thad's chin appeared on the ledge of the rock, then his long neck, and finally, after his elbow caught the ledge, he crawled on top of the hump.

"The map never said that . . ." Thad muttered, trying to collect his arms and legs.

"Map?" Jerry looked at him. His lower arms were stinging and wet. "I thought this cave was all a hunch, Whiteford."

Thad dropped his head into his shoulders.

"Some hunch, cripe." Jerry laughed up at the ceiling and started to make his way back toward the mouth of the cave when he heard a scuffling outside. He instinctively put his arm across Chris who had started picking at his mandolin and he stared down Peter's munching. Slowly, he drew his finger over his mouth. But the scuffling came closer; it came from hefty shoes, something big. The shoes—boots?—seemed uncertain about what they were looking for, but clearly they were looking.

Jerry didn't breathe. He didn't even move his eyes, his eyelashes. Then he saw a set of orange paniers— bulging orange paniers—drop to the side of the cave's mouth, and a Frye boot pause next to it.

"Partini!"

Partini ducked in. "Hey, hey. You trying to avoid me?" he said. "Nice place you have here. A little damp. Can't be good for the sinuses, but . . ."

Jerry's eyes were focused on the paniers and this time he didn't feel like ignoring his suspicions.

"You didn't happen to go into town?" he started, angrily.

"He did," Thad announced, undoubtedly happy to refocus the attention. "Look at those paniers. Empty yesterday and now, poof!"

"Just a little magic," Partini patted one, "and a good sense of humor. For laughs, you know?" He took out a package of pink Hostess cupcakes and put it across his dripping chest: "Size 42, triple cup. Nibble my ear, baby," he whispered to Jerry.

"Where'd you get the money for that?" Before Partini could protect it, Jerry grabbed the panier and unstrapped the pocket. It was jammed with potato chips, two Clark bars, a bottle of Coca-Cola, a bottle of Perrier water, three hard rolls.

"All right, Partini, where did you get the money?"

"A little of mine, a little of ours. Just for a little lightening of the mood . . . or can The Great Sebastian get a joke?"

Jerry emptied the packet on the rocks, a package of TicTacs rolled into a crevice. "Our $5.00?"

Partini shrugged again and held out his palm with a crumpled green bill and some change on it. "There's $1.20 left . . ." When Jerry looked up at the ceiling of the dripping cave, Partini went on, "I ran out of food."

"The first night," Thad helped him.

"So, the first night."

"That's why all the stops," Jerry said.

"So? What do we need money for? Gas?"

Jerry turned away from the emptied paniers and crawled toward the opening of the cave. "I've got to get some air," he said. "It stinks in here," but as he turned, he saw a yellow skirt, drooping heavily with water, and Mimi, in her peasant blouse, crouching under the lip of the ledge.

So. Easy towpath tunnel. Maybe they hadn't fooled Morelli after all. Bull was probably on the thruway to Washington by now.

9

For an hour or more no one really talked. Thunder ripped the sky open, and a slice of lightning chased it before the rumbling had even finished. Light reached into the corners of the mouth of the cave, while outside the wind stirred violent whirlpools of rain and leaves, and the Potomac boiled. The storm had a life all its own. Everyone huddled in the cave, waiting but not speaking.

Then, as quickly as it had started, the ripping turned into a rumble and a lower rumble, and the thundering clouds stalked away to some other woods. The rain became merely now-and-then drops on the rocks, the trees stopped shushing, and Jerry took his paniers and crawled outside.

There was no moon. Cloud giants had left behind them a gray mist, but it was light enough for him to look around. And listen. But he heard nothing. He suspected he couldn't stay with the others, survival or not, but for now he had to sleep. His bike, which he had thrown quickly under the bushes, was drenched, but as he unhooked the bungi cords holding his sleeping bag, the plastic covering felt intact. A soft occasional drop of water fell on his back from the sagging branches. Once in Vermont when he had hiked alone to the mouth of Missisquoi Bay, he had run into a three-day rain. At night in his sagging tent he used to pretend he was a trumpet, just to hear his own voice.

Now he quickly unrolled the tent piece and drew the center ropes from one tree to another in the grove at the edge of the rocks. Then he took the side ropes and stretched them, too, to small trees. His foam he threw out on the drenched soil beneath the cover and unrolled his sleeping bag on it. He really had to sleep.

He had thrown his still sopping sneakers under his bag when he heard a rustling by the cave. A long-haired silhouette crawled toward him.

"Jerry?"

Jerry turned. He knew it was Chris.

"We can get off early tomorrow."

Jerry knew Chris was throwing him a bone. He shrugged. It really was too late.

"Just let them know what you want."

Jerry sat down on the rock and shook his head. "Why don't you tell them what *you* want, for Pete's sake?"

"Hey, man, look at me. They want a hero. Do I look like it?" Chris's pants and shirt, drenched with water, stuck to him and his long wet hair, not banded back now, fell in wet strings over his shoulders. He held his mandolin out over his knee, and grinned. "I'm just the bard."

56

Morelli did have a way of creeping into this trip. Always a hero. Always a dragon. Now it was a bard.

"Look, I am really fed up with this Morelli game. Partini was right the first day. This is the real world, Chris. There are no express tunnels that whisk a flock of heroes to some wondrous place. There's just this rain-drenched mess. Hunches turn out to be maps. And heroes? Well, there's Partini who spends all but $1.20 in less than two days. If there were any heroes maybe we wouldn't have to pretend hunches and look for magic." He looked at Chris. "You want the truth? I'm fed up. I want out."

Chris stretched his legs and pulled his fingers across the mandolin strings. "Maybe heroes don't start out heroes."

"Shit." Jerry shook his head and looked at the still-raging Potomac. A large drop of water from a branch fell on his shoulder and found a crooked path down his arm.

"Morelli didn't promise magic or express tunnels or . . ."

Jerry shrugged.

"Maybe this is just Mirkwood, something tough to get through."

Jerry laughed as he looked around at the grotesquely drooping trees around them. It seemed a lot like Mirkwood tonight. "I'm going, Chris. Sorry."

"And Morelli didn't really say Mirkwood would be good or bad.'"

"Look, Chris, you can do it alone. We didn't see a human being all day, and maybe it was a little rough but at least there are no . . ."

"Dragons?"

"All right, dragons. The tunnel keeps them out."

Chris pursed his lips as if he had some doubts.

"What?" Jerry asked.

"What if one did get into the tunnel?"

Jerry watched him rubbing his chin thoughtfully against the neck of his mandolin.

"The tunnel could also keep one *in* and . . ." He looked up at Jerry. "We'd be trapped with it, wouldn't we?"

"You're talking about the motorcycles."

Chris shrugged maybe.

"Why would they come this far? This isn't their turf."

"I don't know why."

Jerry looked across the river. On the other side a dot of light moved slowly alongside the bank. Maybe a car. It made him crazy that they had to waste time worrying about the motorcycle creeps instead of how to catch up to Bull. Cripe.

"What're we going to do with Mimi?"

"Not 'we,' Chris, 'you' or 'they.' "

Chris made the mandolin whine by drawing his index finger down the length of a string. "She's a real gypsy, isn't she?"

An enchantress now: every journey had one. Morelli, Morelli, Morelli. Jerry shook his head: negative. "No more games."

"Okay, okay, so you're not interested." Chris paused to work his way through a melody of sorts. "Her parents are farm workers, gone planting in upstate New York. She lives in Indian Pool with her older brother until her parents send for them. That's the word."

"If we—or you—can trust her."

"I'm for giving it a whirl, buddy," Chris said as he

placed and replaced his fingers in different positions on the frets of the mandolin.

"If I were going with you, I'd be against letting her come," Jerry said. Chris had lapsed into a sequence of picked runs that sounded twangy like a harpsichord and Jerry muttered.

"A dollar-twenty left. We'd have to divide our food with Partini and Mimi . . . How could he bring only one day of food for a four- or five-day trip? Some canned Spam, anything."

"Hey, buddy," Chris didn't look up but went on picking, "I'm nearly out of food, too."

Jerry laughed. "I figured those flat sacks couldn't have much in them."

Chris shrugged and started humming.

"How long you been at Lockewood?" Jerry asked him.

"Forever. My father teaches in the lower school."

"You seem comfortable," Jerry said.

"Yeh, I guess I am. You?"

"I guess I've got some explosions left in me."

"Maybe we all do." Chris started humming again.

Jerry suddenly lay down. "Why don't you sing for God's sake. Humming won't get us out of anything."

"Us?" He looked up. "I don't sing. I hum."

Jerry grinned. "Great. A hungry bard who doesn't sing. Figures."

"All right, all right." Chris stopped and pondered for a moment.

*'Poor boys,' said the wizard, 'they've neither
bones . . . [he was fishing for words] nor sinew,
they don't know a dragon from a snake, but*

give them wheels to go on,
give them one orange tie,
and give them a gypsy girl to dance them
stories, and they'll ride.'

He was picking his way and Jerry nodded tolerantly, grinning.

"Verse number two," Chris began.

'Poor boys,' said the wizard,
'they've neither bones nor sinew
they haven't any heroes, though they've
tried, but give them wheels to go on . . .'

He looked at Jerry who filled in, "'. . . *give them some canned Spam . . .'"*

Chris laughed, "'*and maybe they'll figure a dragon from a snake.'"*

Jerry scoffed genially. "Some bard, it doesn't rhyme."

Chris went into a fit of glissandos and ended with a magnificent two-string strum. "All right," Jerry agreed. "You're a bard!"

For a moment Chris sat with his mandolin bowl cradled in his arms. "You coming with us tomorrow?" he asked.

"Maybe."

Chris shrugged and crawled into his patched sleeping bag; it couldn't have been waterproof.

When Jerry put his legs into his own bag he was suddenly glad it was dry, and that he had packed the foam-rubber ground cover. Only minutes passed before, curled in his mummy bag, he felt himself fall off into some dark hole, thick and warm.

It must have been nearly daybreak when something woke him, maybe a sound, maybe a dream, he couldn't catch the edges of it. He turned over and stared down the towpath. The clouds had moved off, and shadows breathed across it, but there was nothing there. What was bugging him then? But it was no use. Whatever it was was gone. He was just left with the clear impression that Chris had something—the towpath could be an express tunnel or it could be a trap. In order to really race Bull again, they would have to get by the few villages along the path quickly. No one must know they were there. He had no choice but to stay.

10

In the morning the sandy soil of the towpath, drenched
from the all-night rain, was covered with puddles and
strewn with branches and leaves, but sun sprinkled
across it, and it seemed more like a country lane than
a raging tunnel. But Jerry remembered. Get past towns
quickly and without being seen. He didn't talk about it
—with this group they'd go hyper—he just pulled on
his Lockewood shirt quickly and waited for someone
else to get everybody going.

But no one did. It was like the garbage at home.
Everyone left it to pile higher and higher until the
orange peels started falling on the floor, then Jerry
would finally have to take it out. When Partini leisurely
started hanging his mirror out on a sapling for his
morning shave and Chris started muttering about two
mandolin strings which had swollen in the night, Jerry
knew it was the garbage again.

"Let's go, okay?" he prodded.

"Okay, okay," Partini said, hustling in a mock shuffle. Mimi hung back on her paint-chipped, no-speed red Schwinn, as far away from Jerry she could stay, but Jerry ignored her and sat down with Thad at the map site.

"I say, get near Harpers Ferry for lunch, pass by Brunswick, and stay this side of Seneca tonight. About fifty miles. Washington, tomorrow." Past towns and fast. It sounded easy enough. "We've still got a chance to nose out Bull."

"Agreed, Jerry," Thad bobbed, as he tried to refold a new flat map he had unearthed back into its proper folds. He couldn't find them and started again.

"And food." Jerry looked directly at Partini. "We lay it all out, divide it. Partini, you take lunches; Thad, breakfasts; I'll take dinners."

Thad had started to refold the map for the third time. "And no one touches the $1.20 unless we all agree," Thad added.

"That's a very good idea, Thad, very good," Peter fawned. There was something about his always agreeing that was hard to take.

Partini sprayed his deodorant around everyone's feet, their packs, even the bikes. "And Mimi?" he said without stopping.

Jerry looked at Chris. "How about she rides with us to Brunswick and gets off there," Chris offered.

"A very good town, a train town," Thad broke in.

"But she leaves quickly," Jerry said. "If it's a good-sized town, it's a good town to get by fast." He didn't explain.

Some people called the canal "the ditch" and that is what it looked like as they walked their bikes up to it.

Empty of water here, it was filled with sodden leaves from the night before. Jerry wrapped an empty bread bag around his seat, tied it, then pushed his bike out onto the towpath. What they could use was a good day —a fast day. Suddenly Jerry realized he'd give his lunch —maybe dinner too—to know where Bull Templeton was. But the hard-packed sand of the day before had moistened and turned spongy. Bicycling out first, Jerry tried to set his tire on the sloping edge, a harder edge. No good. He jumped his bike over into the grass strip, and the five bikes tottered over in a line behind him, all of them searching for a firmer groove. But there they discovered the broken branches. And splinters.

Peter got the first one—a blowout caused by a two-inch branch spear—less than two miles from the cave. He had a repair kit, but Thad stayed with him. Partini got the second one trying to jump his bike over a tiny limb of leaves. He had an extra tube, but had never changed a tire.

"I hate sweat," he groaned as Jerry and Chris stopped to change his tire for him. "The smell of it is enough to make me vomit." He started spraying his deodorant around the bike as they worked.

Even Chris did not escape. On a patch of clear path, no leaves, no branches, five minutes after helping Partini, Chris's back tire simply went slowly flat. "Go ahead," he called to Jerry. "Mimi's going back to check Gollum. We'll catch up at Harpers Ferry."

Jerry took them up on it. All right, he wouldn't go off alone to Washington, but he had played hero all morning, planning, changing tires, and statistically, three flats should be their limit.

A funny thing about pedaling out alone: if you

pedaled far enough ahead you couldn't hear what was happening behind you. He almost made a game of the branches that lay across the path. Lifting his wheels over some, jumping over others with the whole bike, swerving in neat patterns around others. Lock 36. Lock 35. The clock he heard was his own. They had agreed: Harpers Ferry by noon. He'd get there—no problem. When the towpath suddenly broke into an opening, he didn't even stop to walk out on the rocks that lay like basking turtles on the side of the river. His clock was ticking.

"Move it!" he shouted out loud. He was the wind, and by eleven-thirty he saw the town of Harpers Ferry clinging to its hillside spot as the trees thinned around it. The Potomac and Shenandoah rivers crashed together, churning over the rocks in low falls that cut deeply into the green-treed valley. But he wouldn't go near the town.

He left his bike and walked over the rocks. The sound of the tumbling water whispered in his ears. Somehow it was fresh, maybe because he was hearing it alone. He found a rock where he could leave his bike, and lie in the sun like one more turtle. Lazily he thought, we'll get past Brunswick: zip. Forty miles to Seneca: zip. No problem.

But the others didn't come. The sun tilted off its center position—it had to be twelve—but no one came. He started ticking off possibilities. They couldn't have gotten more than three flats. They hadn't passed a town. They hadn't heard anything suspicious this morning. They hadn't even seen another human being. The towpath wasn't really Mirkwood: the others could make it alone.

The sun tilted farther, drying the salt on his skin. Jerry licked his upper arm, stretched out again and listened. All he heard was a far-off mournful train whistle. He looked down the path. Nothing. No one. Then, after counting to eighty-five, a particular number he always picked when he was waiting for something, he got up. It was the garbage again.

He met Mimi just as he pedaled back onto the path. She had tied her blouse in a knot at her middle, and beads of sweat curled in the hair pushed back off her ears.

"Partini had another flat. Thad had two, and Gollum's got a problem . . ."

Jerry put up his hand to stop her. He wheeled his bike back on the towpath. "Spare me, okay? Just stay here." Besides him, she was the only one who hadn't gotten a flat—and on her broken-down Schwinn—but flat or no flat, if they could get rid of her, it would make his day.

11

It was strangely quiet cycling back alone because he was pedaling with the wind, not against it, and there was an eerie absence of noise. Just the whirr of his own wheels. Jerry found himself watching the woods that opened up like a parting green sea before him at the sides of the canal and towpath. But as he pedaled into the second mile back, he met no one. He came to the spot near Lock 36 where he had left Chris, but he wasn't there. Another mile down the road, he passed a scuffled spot in the middle of the path and Partini's potato-chip wrapper, but no Partini. Then he heard a rattling kind of whirr behind him and turned to see Mimi catching up. She wasn't even good at taking advice.

But that was the only noise he heard until he turned a bend at the end of a farmer's field. Then a peal of laughter broke around the curve and an announcement: "That is stupid, Gollum!" It could only be Partini.

Jerry coasted up to the clearing. Chris seemed to be staring at a fallen tree. Partini, sitting on a small concrete fragment, had his back to whatever it was Chris was watching. Jerry braked with his feet and tried to figure out what was happening. A barbed-wire fence on the opposite side of the canal had been crushed by a tremendous thick-barked tree which had obviously fallen in the night since the lightning slice still oozed sap. The leaves of it scattered over the dry canal and path for some distance around. But at the point where the tree lay across the fence, there was a brown animal, the color of a deer but smaller, caught in a tangle of the wire. Peter was lying on his belly next to it.

"Unbelievable, isn't it," Partini shouted. "Chickens, now rabbits. I present Gollum, our incomparable gift to the veterinarian societies of the world."

Jerry quickly glanced down the tunnel—still empty —then walked to the edge of the canal. It was a rabbit all right, but the biggest one he had ever seen. As still as if it were dead, it lay pinned between wire and tree, its neck caked with blood and twisted peculiarly against a slight rise. The dark black eyes stared. It looked dead.

Peter ignored Jerry and snipped away at the piece of wire pinned flat by the tree. Suddenly the rabbit started to kick, flapping its legs and pulling frantically against the wire. Then it lay still again.

"Brave little bugger," Chris said. "He won't give up."

"Come on, Gollum. We've been here twenty minutes!" Partini shouted. When there was no response, he shook out a small mat and sat on it. "These leaves are going to set my allergy off. I just hope I have enough vitamin C. You'll pay, Gollum, if not!"

"Can it, Partini," Jerry said, but he glanced down the empty towpath again. He tried to inch closer, but Peter waved him away.

The difficulty was clear. The double wires, one on top of the rabbit and one below, formed a kind of trap. When the rabbit pulled back, the spikes of the wire caught it. When it tried to push through, it ran into the tree-crushed bank. It had started to kick again. Peter stroked it until its panicky eyes fell back into a stare. Obviously, its hind leg had been cut, too, by the lower wire. Peter snipped again at the top wire, but he was using bike pliers and they weren't enough to cut. Still he snipped. The rabbit twinged as the twist forced the wire into its neck.

"He looks so frightened," Mimi whispered.

"I don't think Gollum can get him out," Chris said.

Peter snipped again, but the rabbit started kicking and flailing, its back feet beating the air, finally catching Peter's wrist.

"See!" Partini muttered, holding his nose. "You do a rabbit a good turn, and that's what you get. One of my oldest mottos is: never help a rabbit. You'll probably get blood poisoning and die a ghastly death."

Peter snipped.

"Let nature take care of its own, I say." Partini had taken out the group's lunch pack. "And what about his family life? Rabbits know humans stink. Once the family smells a human on a relative, it's all over. No family. No friends. Destined to travel the towpath alone."

Chris and Jerry watched Peter working silently. Now the rabbit was squealing softly, not moving, just squealing. Peter winced as he reached into his panier, took out an antiseptic and sprayed it onto the leg and neck. The rabbit, strangely, did not fight it.

"That is disgusting," Partini said.

Peter had gone over to the tree, whispered something to Thad, then reached around the smaller, higher part of the trunk with his tremendous arms.

"Ready?" he asked Thad. Thad tucked his lips in and held his spidery hands around the rabbit as Peter sucked in a breath and lifted. There was a murmur of leaves, but the tree didn't budge.

"Hey, wait a minute," Jerry called out, but Peter had already reached again around the trunk, nearly encircling it with his arms. A grunt squeezed out of him as he strained. Jerry ran toward him but Peter had already lifted the tree a sliver of light off the ground, and the rabbit that had been listlessly lying there, suddenly came to life.

Thad squeezed his hands closed, but the rabbit shot forward, under the wire, and as Thad scrambled to corner it, the rabbit spun around and dashed the other way. Thad tumbled backwards trying to snatch it, his long legs no help to him at all. When the rabbit found Thad strung out in front of it, it turned and floundered into their two bikes, which crashed down upon each other and fell over onto the edge of the canal, narrowly missing the fleeing animal.

Jerry thrust his hand out to catch the rabbit, but it gave several midair kicks at him and turned down the empty towpath, its white tail flicking the air as it raced away.

"I'm sorry," Thad said sheepishly.

Partini sneezed. "Fur," he said. "Nasty little rodent."

But Peter grinned. "He's not dead," he said. However, when he and Thad disentangled their bikes, Peter shouted across at Jerry. "The screw's gone."

Jerry called back, "That's okay. I have extras." He reached into his pack.

Peter looked sheepish. "This is a Raleigh. A British standard screw's missing. Metric won't work."

"You can't ride without it?" Jerry asked.

Peter shook his head no.

Jerry could feel the heat rising in his neck. "No one has a British screw? Partini?"

"What's a screw?"

"Thad?"

"Sorry," he bobbed his head into his shoulders. "We've only one patch left too . . . There's a bike shop in Brunswick."

"Brunswick!" He just stared at Thad, then added quietly, "Okay, Peter, Thad, you start walking . . . I'll go ahead to Brunswick for the screw and patches."

"With me," Chris said and threw his leg over the bar.

"And me," Mimi said. Yes, that was what he needed; a stubborn thirteen-year-old tagging along. Brunswick he wasn't going to look forward to, but at least they could get rid of her that much faster.

12

"Brunswick used to be a noisy canal town fifty years ago," Mimi shouted ahead.

Jerry didn't answer her. Her ridiculous thick old Schwinn was built more like a tank than a bike, but somehow she kept up.

"That was before the railroad came through," she went on. "Kids still like the place."

"Kids?" Jerry threw back over his shoulder.

"You know, locals, hikers . . . bikers . . ."

Sometimes he had the feeling she knew what was worrying him, but a TOWN OF BRUNSWICK sign saved him from probing that idea. Beyond the next turn, the towpath ran into a clearing, and at a spot where the canal and railroad nearly touched, a lonely railroad station huddled alongside a road that led into town. As they pulled up, Jerry could see the heat rise in waves over the hot cement bridge that crossed the canal. He really didn't want to go into that town.

"I'll go for the screw and patches," Mimi said as she coasted forward. She had pedaled all morning in that longish yellow peasant skirt. As impractical as Partini.

"No," Jerry said and looked away from her. "Chris and I'll go."

"Wait, I really want to go and," she hesitated, "I know the town a little, where people hang out and . . ."

"No. You tell the others where we are. When we get back you make your call home and . . ."

"You know, I may not be Lockewood Academy, but did it ever occur to you I might help?"

He started rolling forward. "I could go anyway, whether you want me to or not!" she said, as he passed. For a moment they stared at each other. Her eyes were bottomless black.

"You could," Jerry finally said, but after another moment she looked away from him and, pulling her skirts angrily around her, sat on the concrete and dangled her feet impatiently over the edge.

But it was easy for Jerry to ignore her. The only idea in his head was to get into town and get out. He and Chris pedaled past the train station. It smelled of greasy mail sacks thrown onto the walk. An antique luggage cart stood empty in front of the door. At the first street, they turned toward town.

It took two inquiries to find the tiny shop, which stood almost alone in a field at the edge of town. Wheels hung in the window like spindled sausages, along with a hand-sketched sign that read, "Be back at two." An old dusty school clock on the back wall said 1:20. Cripe. Jerry sat on the weedy curb and looked around him. The whole town looked as if it were asleep. Not a soul moved, not even in the gas station

73

across the field. Then in the distance he saw shingled village roof tops and, above them, seats dangling at the top of a gigantic Ferris wheel.

"Why not?" Chris said behind him. "Forty minutes to wait. Let's take a look."

Jerry shook his head. Sometimes he used to wander at small town carnivals in Vermont when one came through. There was a kind of magic about them, even though they were honky-tonk. But now? No way would he go now.

"It'll take Peter and Thad an hour to get here walking," Chris said, "and, look, do we really want to sit in front of this empty field where we can be seen for a half-mile?"

"It's off the track, Chris!" Just when they had decided where the track was. "Let's go back."

"With no screws or patches?" Chris tucked his mandolin in his pack and coasted into the street. "Come on, let's take a look."

Jerry found himself glancing over his shoulder as the two of them coasted down the slight hill to the end of the block, then pedaled toward the Ferris wheel. It kept appearing and disappearing, first behind a hotel, then behind a steepled church. Following it, they finally turned and pedaled into the main street. At a dead end, the carnival seemed to spring up like a noisy weed.

It was strictly small time. At the entrance, hand-lettered signs shouted in red paint: TWO-HEADED BABY CAN TALK TO ITSELF, 200-YEAR-OLD JUNGLE MAN EATS LIVE CHICKENS, and MONSTER CROCODILES. The two chained their bikes to a lead-pipe railing and walked past the signs over the still rain-soaked grass. Wires ran across the field like snakes, connecting a kiddy-car merry-go-round with a noisy generator. A giant, air-filled jumping square swayed as kids inside squealed and fell over each other. At a booth, another swarm of kids egged on a mouse who, let go, frantically dashed for a hole to crawl into.

"Like us, huh?" Chris grinned, as an elderly man with a white panama hat moved nervously away from him. The long hair again, probably.

The carnival made Jerry jumpy. Just as the town had. That might be why, when he heard sounds over the Zipper Ride, he instantly thought they were motorcycle sounds. He jerked around, but all he saw was a young mother trying to persuade two under-five-year-olds that the miniature fire engine would be the best car to choose. Between Gollum and his bleeding rabbit, six flats, and the tunnel . . . paranoid, that's what he was. Why would Pennsylvania motorcyclists bother to ride a hundred miles to smear a few bicyclists anyway. It didn't even make sense to him.

But after he and Chris watched squealing riders bash their cars through a Dodgem course, they turned past a pony ring. When Jerry lifted his head, straight ahead, he saw three motorcycles parked next to their bikes. One of the cycles was yellow with a chrome snake exhaust.

He jerked his head toward Chris.

"I saw them," Chris said.

"It's impossible."

"I know."

Jerry let his eyes search the grounds, slowly and carefully. Finally he caught sight of the back of three black-helmeted cyclists, sitting with the operator of the Tilt-o-Whirl.

"Let's get out of here," Jerry said without moving his lips. But the Tilt-o-Whirl sat between them and their bikes.

"Where?" Chris asked.

Jerry looked around. Open rides. Open booths. Open fields. But they couldn't wait there like sitting ducks.

Barely moving, Chris nudged him. "How much money do we have?" he whispered. Jerry put out the $1.20 in his palm, and Chris nodded at the sign in front of them: MOON WALK 50¢. "It'll buy us time," he said. The back of Jerry's neck burned.

"No! We said we had to agree on the $1.20 . . ."

"Jerry!"

He turned. The cyclists had stood up and started looking slowly around the fairgrounds with their helmet-eyes.

It was Ed Anderson all over again.

13

It was like a huge yellow bubble with oval windows all around the sides. Jerry ducked in in his stocking feet, each foot sinking into a pillow of air as if he had dropped into a cloud. Reluctantly leaving his mandolin at the door with the carny operator, Chris followed him. But every time Chris took a step, Jerry felt himself being puffed up. Suddenly, Chris jumped behind him and when he landed, Jerry felt himself being thrown bodily into the air. He scrambled to hang onto something, but five little kids, nine years old or so, enjoying his quandary, jumped around him in a ring. He felt himself rolling helplessly into the ravines they created.

The crazy kids had probably been jumping here all day. They knew how to take each swell. Chris tried to jump to the other side of the bubble, but three of the kids, laughing hysterically, stalked him. Two others, one with fiery red hair, jumped on either side of Jerry, rocking him from side to side. Jerry caught himself at the first sideways swell, almost fell to the other side as it snapped up on him, then drifted helplessly into a sudden hole.

He had tumbled into it hands first, when Chris, running around behind him, shouted, "Check the ovals!" Three of the not-quite-clear ovals were filled with helmet-eyes. The question was, through the distorting plastic, how much did they see?

After a glance, Jerry, suddenly laughing, jumped as if he hadn't seen anything. Shrieks of the other kids jumping and laughing filled the cavernous bubble. "Do they recognize us?" Jerry shouted through a smile.

Chris came running over in strange slow-motion steps and jumped next to him. "I don't know."

As Jerry sent his arm out behind him to catch himself, he saw the faces still there, one of them saying something, maybe shouting something. He couldn't hear. The small redheaded kid in coveralls came up behind him and jumped him into a rear tumble, but Jerry landed on his feet this time.

"There's no way out," Jerry said. The smile on his face was as painted as Partini's party face.

"I know." Chris's long hair swung up as he jumped and landed, but now behind him, Jerry saw the faces were gone. This had been a stupid move. It hadn't bought any time at all. Jerry took huge bounding steps to the windows, all in that slow motion as if he had been thrown into another world; even his arms came down to his sides in slow motion. His breath, slow motion.

The redhead came at him again, in short bounces, laughing all the time like a hyena, bouncing at his side, then as Jerry caught himself, bouncing behind him, each time jumping back to a safe mountain away from Jerry. Jerry let himself drop low into the giant pillow but when he came up, he flew across the mound toward the little boy. All he could see was a toothy grin. Jerry came down with all his weight, but laughing hysterically, the red-haired brat jumped into the air out of his reach.

Chris pulled Jerry's shirt. At the doorway, stepping in in their stocking feet, were the three cyclists. Helmets still on. Chris had to leave his mandolin but they could wear their helmets! They had thrown off their jackets and were down to cut-off black sweat shirts. The three of them looked the same to Jerry. Like giant black insects. That was a terrible thought, but they looked the same, and the three of them were coming toward them, not bouncing, but stalking.

The sweat broke out on Jerry's cheeks and along the rims of his glasses. He looked behind himself and Chris. They were caught, wedged in one of the corners farthest from the door, but only if they stayed there. Pulling his elbows in to his waist, Jerry jumped, tumbling Chris into his footsteps, but rippling the trapped air across the bubble floor and finally blowing out a pillow in front of the cyclists that threw them off balance. Two tumbled into a rolling spiral. The third caught himself and pushed off toward them. Jerry glanced to his right. Chris was crawling to the wall of the bubble.

But a cyclist with a light wispy mustache had gotten to his feet and was staring with his one helmet eye at Jerry, alone in the corner. Somehow Jerry was certain it was the yellow cyclist. Again, Jerry threw his elbows into his sides and plunged into the pillow, but this time the cyclist put his fingertips back in time to catch himself. He moved closer. Another one-eye walked around the wave's crest to join him. Jerry backed up and started jumping again and again, sending waves of air swelling at them.

Tumbling briefly toward each other, they caught themselves and thrust themselves into Jerry's half of the bubble. Chris had made it to the corner nearest the door. Behind their backs, he motioned toward the tiny exit. But there was no way for Jerry to get there. The three of them spanned the bubble and were slowly jumping toward him like moon walkers with no gravity pull. They moved closer and closer. Jerry looked for a hole between them—it appeared to be the only way past them—when suddenly, he felt a red streak fling itself in front of the cyclists, jumping high into the air and plummeting down, then leaping up again. It was the red-haired brat, laughing and jumping in front of them, giving Jerry just time enough to roll sideways across to the windows. There he sprang to his feet, feeling some power in his legs, while the redhead weaved between the stumbling cyclists like a crazy laughing bee.

Jerry jumped in a spanning leap toward the door, across the moon. He could see the three black figures trying to recover their balance on the pillow behind him, but, as Chris slipped down onto solid ground to collect his mandolin, Jerry slipped down beside him.

Outside, the ground wouldn't stop swelling. Jerry's knees buckled as he tried to make it stop, but after he bent over in the rocking world to pick up his shoes, he stood up to see a man in a deep-blue suit staring at him.

"Just follow me you two," the man said, as Jerry caught sight of one of the cyclists backing away from the door.

14

Jerry and Chris stepped over the wire cables that ran across this half of the fairgrounds like a nest of snakes. Their sneakers sank into the wet ground. At a tiny paint-chipped shack at the edge of the grounds, the policeman nudged them into a doorway, and, as he switched a light on, they could see a totally empty room. It smelled of wet wood.

"Where you kids from?" He looked suspiciously at Jerry's Lockewood tee shirt.

"Pennsylvania," Jerry said, quickly turning his voice to a gentler tone. "What's the trouble, sir? We . . ."

"Hey! Like TV says, I'll tell you when to say something." His thick upper lip curled at them. "I don't like you guys very much."

Jerry blew up into his curls. This was really funny. Jerry Sebastian, the quiet kid in the corner who never bothered anyone, who ran his track, went on his hikes

82

and never got in any trouble in his life. Funny, that's what it was.

Chris wisely stayed quiet.

"You kids from all over come into this town and make trouble."

"Trouble? We paid . . ." but Jerry stopped himself as the man looked up angrily at him.

The policeman had short, crew-cut hair, and looked more like a Marine sergeant than a local cop. His thick jaw worked energetically over a wad of tobacco, but his badge and buttons were shined, number 324 etched clearly on the lower edge.

"First off, we don't allow bicycles on the thruway here."

Jerry looked at Chris.

"We weren't on any thruway . . . sir," Jerry said.

"And don't lie. We got a call on you Lockewood kids this morning."

"But this morning . . . ?"

Bull Templeton! The cop must have gotten a call on Templeton and those guys. Racing their heads off on the thruway!

"And I saw the trouble you were causing in the bubble, getting the little kids stirred up." Jerry settled back. Dumb jerk. One shirt was the same as another, one big kid was the same as another. He hoped his disgust wasn't obvious.

"You're a real smart-ass, aren't you." The policeman caught Jerry's sleeve and flicked it. Then he looked with equal disgust at Chris's hair and frayed, gray shirt. Chris leaned back against the wall clutching his mandolin, with absolutely no expression on his face. He just stared.

"Where are the rest of you?"

Jerry worked his tongue up alongside his teeth and tried to look neutral. That would be all they would need: to have the police find they had a strange thirteen-year-old kid with them. A girl. Maybe a runaway. Jerry nervously rubbed the sweat off his top lip.

The policeman dropped his palm against the opposite wall, hard.

"The rest!" he said again. All Jerry could see were huge teeth.

"Trouble with you kids, you have too much. Your Lockewood academies. Why aren't you in school like other kids anyway?" His teeth were big and yellow, mule teeth. Jerry could feel Chris beginning to perspire next to him where their arms touched. A clock, the only piece of furniture in the room, read 2:00. Ironic, they were being held while Templeton breezed his way to Washington on an expressway. Ironic, the bicycle shop was open and they couldn't get there.

The policeman smacked the wall again, louder, when suddenly, the handle of the shack turned and a youngish, thin policeman with small round glasses pushed his way in.

"What's this?" He had a soft voice that sounded as if it wound through his nose.

"The Lockewood kids. Boy, you've got a memory. You heard the call."

Now the younger policeman hit the wall. "You sure that's them? Short hair, the call said. Short hair, blue helmets, all Lockewood shirts."

"The call could be wrong about hair. How can you see hair under helmets anyway?"

The younger man flicked Chris's pony tail and

plucked his gray shirt. "You can't hide that and that." He paused, then looked up at Jerry. "You been on the thruway?"

Jerry shook his head. "Towpath."

He studied Jerry's eyes for a moment, then turned to the older policeman. "Cripe, Brady, how can you get kids mixed up?"

"Lockewood is Lockewood."

The younger policeman paced to the end of the shack and stood there.

"Well, it comes to the same thing to me," the older cop said. "I don't want strange kids hanging around here." He turned to Jerry, placing his face almost next to Jerry's. Jerry could smell his breath. "You take your smart-ass looks, get on your bikes, and you get out of this town, hear? We don't want your type around here. And you stay off the thruway or you'll spend the night in jail while your parents come and get you. That'd embarrass you big shots. Understand?"

Jerry was afraid to move, as if any movement would send the policeman off on another wild tack. But the policeman suddenly stood up straight. "Lockewood Academy. Bullshit."

Jerry cautiously stepped out of the shack's door into blinding sun. But there was a final irony. As he and Chris checked the railing, they discovered their bikes were still there, but the cycles had disappeared. Jerry let his eyes search each building, each ride, the faces of each carny operator he could see—kids, old men—but the cyclists were gone.

"Hey, man, the cop saved us," Chris whispered as they started toward their bikes.

"I think he'd be disappointed if he knew," Jerry whispered back without turning toward Chris.

But they had only walked a few steps when the older policeman threw the door open. "Hey," he shouted, "keep off the towpath, too. The aqueduct is out at Catoctin, and the river's high."

15

Jerry stood in the nook of the bike-shop doorway rolling the dime in his hands. For a dime the owner had given them a screw "Not quite the right size but it should hold," and two extra patches. They had a single dime left. But that wasn't their biggest problem. What did the cop mean the aqueduct was out. How could it be out? That left only small highways or backroads, perfect road set-ups for cyclists or any other dragons. Something Templeton had obviously not had to face.

The high whine of a train moaned across the field. The store owner inside reached up toward the clock and moved the hands back. 3:05. Chris was sitting on the curb, contentedly working out some strange new melody.

"Wonder how the train gets over the river," Chris muttered as he went on picking. He hardly seemed to notice he had said anything.

Jerry stared at him for a long moment.

"What did you say?" Jerry asked.

"Nothing," Chris said.

"You wondered how the train gets over the river," Jerry said.

"Oh." Chris was frowning over his fingering.

A slow grin worked its way across Jerry's lips, and he started to nod his head. "Yeh," he said. Still nodding, he went back to the store and opened the door a crack. "When is the next train to Washington?" he said to the shop owner.

"Not until six. Going or coming, not until six," the man said without taking his eyes off a wheel he was straightening.

Jerry quickly returned to his bike, threw his leg over the seat and coasted out while Chris struggled to pack the mandolin, coast out and catch up.

"Remind me to tell you about the day I crawled over the lunchroom ceiling to escape Ed Anderson," Jerry said.

"Who's Ed Anderson?" Chris asked.

"Forget it," Jerry called back.

But at the intersection of the towpath and railroad tracks, the hot pavement that bridged the canal was empty. As Jerry coasted down the towpath, Thad and Peter hiked across a park field toward him, Peter clutching a new addition, a paper bag.

"They've gone on," Thad shouted.

"What do you mean, 'they've'? The girl, too?" Jerry shouted back, glancing suspiciously at the bag. They had agreed no holding out on food. Maybe it was just something left from lunch.

Peter nodded. "Mimi, too," he said.

"Sorry," Thad said. Sometimes Jerry wasn't sure

which of them was sorrier. He personally felt like putting his fist through a tree.

"But they went down the towpath?"

The two nodded together. At least it was in the right direction and Partini and the girl wouldn't go far with the Catoctin aqueduct out.

Quickly, then, they reset the screw in Peter's bike and bent the frame back in line. Jerry gave them a capsule story of the Moon Walk bubble and the police, and the four of them coasted out. Jerry threw a last glance toward Brunswick, letting his eyes travel over the station, the field behind it, the few shops, the streets he could see. There were no specks he could recognize. Or hear. Not from here anyway. If things went right it would be the last time he'd have to care.

Before Brunswick was completely out of sight a government sign posted on a tree warned: CATOCTIN AQUEDUCT OUT, BIKERS, HIKERS USE LOCAL ROADS. Thad dragged his feet to stop and hung his head, but Jerry and Chris passed him.

"Trust us," Jerry shouted, giving his right pedal an extra push. Peter, panting, his new package still unopened and wedged into his basket, brought up the rear. It was frankly difficult to believe Peter hadn't eaten his whole lunch.

They spotted the aqueduct but there was no sign of Mimi and Partini. The canal tunnel opened up into a huge clearing spanned by a 130-foot three-arched aqueduct. The Catoctin. Incredibly, Jerry could almost sense the barges moving out of the trees into the clearing, the mules grunting as they pulled. But the policeman hadn't been lying and Mimi had guessed wrong. When last year's hurricane struck, the aqueduct had crumbled and it hadn't been fixed since. Huge holes torn into its floor revealed the brown and turbulent river below. No one could cross that aqueduct.

Jerry started to search the area as Thad set his bike against a tree and walked as if in a trance to the edge.

"Oh, I don't think I could . . . those holes would . . . well, my feet. . . ."

"No Partini," Chris said after a quick scout of the bank.

"Or Mimi," Peter added. Sweat was oozing out of the thick folds in his neck as he looked around.

But Jerry was looking for something else. Then Chris nudged him and pointed to a hand-painted sign tacked on a tree which said simply: TRESTLE. It hung at a tilt next to a narrow, almost hidden dirt path that led away from the canal through thick brush along the cliff bordering the Catoctin River.

"That's what we're looking for." Grinning, Jerry pulled his bike that way. He listened one more time for sounds behind him, then, hearing none, he started down the path with Chris and Peter behind him.

"Wait!" Thad called out, then after some unexplained rustling he, too, joined them on the path.

Sandy and damp but no longer wet, the trestle path snaked through dense bushes, the branches of which swept across it like arms. Only a spattering of sunlight found its way to the ground at their feet, and mosquitoes swarmed in the leaves. Sorry that he hadn't put his shirt back on after they'd fixed Peter's bike, Jerry tried to avoid the thorny branches, holding one after another for Chris so they wouldn't flip back at him. He could hear Peter behind Chris, panting, stomping right over the thorny maze, while Thad, bringing up the rear, tried to fight the willowy branches, which managed to catch some part of him—if not a sleeve, a pocket—no matter how he tried to avoid them.

At least the path was straight, and for a hundred feet it remained straight, but suddenly, in a small clearing, the path twisted into a runoff gully, sharply falling to the right, then climbing again up the other side in rock-step fashion. Nothing for a backpacker, murder for a biker.

"One at a time," Jerry called back.

"I'll help," Peter said, tumbling up beside them. How? was the question on Jerry's tongue.

"That's all right, Gollum," Chris said. "We'll get it."

The others hunched up behind them as Jerry, moving backwards, let the front wheel of his Peugeot down the steep, twisting trail and Chris guided the back wheel. Jerry's feet felt-touched for solid ground. Chris, his long hair swinging down over his shoulders, blue eyes intent on the wheel he was guiding, hummed all the way. At the bottom they easily carried the bike across the trickle of a stream and started up.

Rock chunks clung to the other side, and as they struggled to find footing, a giant mosquito bit into Jerry's leg. Buzzing dots swarmed at them, bit their shoulders, ears, calves. But they couldn't stop to swat them. Suddenly, a mosquito bit Jerry's cheek, and the ground cropped up at the same time. When Jerry instinctively reached to slap the mosquito away, he stepped into a rubble of rock and started to slip.

"Chris!" he yelled. As he slid, the bike slipped out of his grip, toppling Chris. Bike, Jerry and Chris started to tumble into the gully.

Peter set his paper bag down, dropped his own bike

and started down the hill, catching at the bushes and shoving them aside like an angry bear. At the bottom, he slid into the small stream without thinking, squeegeeing into the mud and rumbling out on the other side. Jerry and Chris had already set the bike at a manageable angle when Peter thundered up and Thad skittered to a stop next to him. The bike started to topple as the two of them scrambled to help, all legs and thumbs.

"We've got it, we've got it," Jerry found himself shouting, as if maybe they wouldn't hear the first time. Gollum and the clumsy wizard: together the two of them were a disaster.

At the top of the ravine, the trail grew lighter. Fewer bushes webbed the path, and finally, lighter and lighter, the trail opened up at a railroad trestle.

The Chesapeake and Ohio train trestle. As neat and tidy as the aqueduct was crumbling, the white stone-carpeted trestle ran narrowly across the deep river. It was a long expanse across.

At first Jerry didn't spot Partini's pink shirt, but when he went back to the path to shout to the others that he had discovered the trestle, he saw Partini sitting in a bower of bushes under the only tree in sight. Next to him, Mimi lay on her back in the sun, adding to her already deep tan. Partini, who had taken off his shoes, was sitting on a plaid cloth, shaving, his mirror hanging in a bush.

No words came to Jerry. Thad came up behind him and stared.

"Well, don't look so shocked, Jerry . . . Wizard. You didn't think we were going to cross that trestle alone, did you? Intelligence, not hunches, is the greater part of valor." He saw Peter lumbering through the opening with his Raleigh, his hair stringy with sweat.

"Eiew!" Partini grimaced and took out the deodorant spray again. "I think there ought to be a decent limit to how much sweat one person can exude."

Zap.

Peter smiled at him. Peter always just smiled at him.

16

Jerry walked to the edge of the trestle. A white rock border three feet wide ran on either side of the tracks, plenty of room to walk a bike when the track was empty. As long as no train came, there should be no difficulty getting across.

"It looks good," Jerry said finally.

"But Jerry," Thad stammered, "there are no warning lights, and the bend at the other end makes vision impossi—"

"The next train is at six," Jerry broke in, "coming or going. But first . . ." He turned to Mimi. "The deal was Brunswick." He still had never called her by name.

She stubbornly bit the corner of her lip.

"Look," Partini cut in. "I told her to come. I insisted, Sebastian. There's nothing at her home right now . . . she's a touch of fragrance on this so-called journey."

Chris had sat down next to his bike. *"Fragrant flower . . ."* he started to sing, *"so-called journey, how I'd like to be back home . . . give me sidewalks . . . give me gas fumes . . . I can't stand mosquito nests."*

"Look," Jerry stared, everyone knew how he felt this time, "she . . ."

"No, you look," Mimi interrupted. "I can talk for myself. All right maybe I'm a pain, but I tried to go to Brunswick . . . oh, forget that. It's too late for me to make it home tonight and . . . I promise this time. I'll go home at Seneca. The highway cuts in there again. I'll call ahead and go home."

Jerry looked at Chris for support, but he seemed to be straining, mouth open, over a chord he had discovered. Thad had sat down cross-legged on the edge of the trestle, the wizard again. "I'll get vibrations," he said pinching the bridge of his nose. But it seemed clear to Jerry, Seneca was one more day. Just postponing things. "No," he said.

"Look, you need someone to go first across the trestle," Mimi was saying. "I'll go and I'll walk down the rails to watch for trains coming the other way. Just in case."

Cripe. That wasn't even worth answering. Jerry turned around to pick up his bike, but Mimi had already walked confidently over to her own no-speed Schwinn, picked it up and started along the track. She didn't rush. Her yellow peasant skirt swung slowly out from her thickish legs. She pushed the bike through the gravel siding with some difficulty, but she pushed it.

"Hey!" Jerry shouted, but she had already started

onto the trestle. Jerry grabbed his bike, knowing he must look like a fool, and started after her. "This is stupid," he shouted ahead to her. "If you're going to ignore . . ." But he knew any threat he leveled at her would sound even more stupid.

It really was impossible pushing his bike through gravel, and the sun on the trestle seemed hotter for the reflecting stones. He could feel the heat through the soles of his shoes.

Mimi's chubby hips moved back and forth as she pushed her bike. She didn't look back.

The trestle had started spanning the deep valley where, far below them, the river burrowed brown and thick through the green trees. In the distance, the crumbling aqueduct stood like an ancient Roman ruin.

"Mimi!"

Still, she didn't turn, and she said nothing either. She just went on pushing across. They were almost halfway when they heard a whistle, something of a curving whistle that seemed to rise up from the trees on the far side. No. Unbelievable. The next train was at six. . . .

Mimi didn't walk any faster, she just pushed steadily along.

"Mimi!" Why was the wind catching his voice? "Can you hear me?"

"Move it, Hero," Partini shouted from the other side.

Jerry started to run his bike. There was not enough room for the train's overhang and the bikes. Not enough. He felt an incredible sweep of heat rushing up through his neck as he ran, pushing the bike over the gravel.

"Faster, Mimi!" he shouted. The whistle blew again whining closer over the trees.

Mimi regripped her handlebars and pushed at the same rate. Jerry had caught up to her rear tire. They were nearly three-quarters of the way over the trestle. Without turning, or losing step, she kept on. Jerry could hear the ticking engine slicing up the railway. He still couldn't see it.

He felt his neck growing hotter. He couldn't pass her, his wheel nicking hers could tumble her, and the fall had to be a hundred feet. "Hurry," he said over the clicking. As they reached the point where the trestle passed over the far bank of the river, the nose of the train rumbled around the bend. But the gravel siding widened slightly here, and as the black monster grumbled toward them, an apron miraculously spread out on either side.

When the noisy giant reached the clearing, Mimi simply guided her Schwinn onto the apron at the same pace, while Jerry flung his bike over behind her. They stood back to watch the hulking black thing rifle past, the box cars streaking by in metallic smears. It seemed endless, snaking across the trestle and into the field beyond. And harmless. No one had interfered.

Jerry's eyes felt hot. Cripe.

Then it occurred to him. Six o'clock for the next passenger train. This had been a freight train.

Finally the noise was gone, except for the whistle approaching Brunswick. "I'll go down the track to watch for any others," Mimi said softly, and she started down the now wide path, her peasant skirt swaying from side to side.

If she was only thirteen, thirteen had changed since he was thirteen. When he looked back, Chris had started across the trestle, with Peter and Partini behind him. Thad brought up the rear.

17

It was Thad who started laughing first. The minute he was across the trestle, he folded himself on the gravel apron next to his bike and started. Jerry dropped his bike and came back to him, Mimi just behind. Peter kept saying. "What is it, Thad?" But just seeing him laugh so hard made Peter start, too, so that he half asked and half laughed, his thick chin bouncing as he tried to remain coherent. Chris grinned from the sideline.

"Sorry, sorry . . ." Thad kept repeating, "It's just . . ." he started laughing again, "It's just that we've outsmarted the dragons."

Jerry stopped laughing.

"Those cyclists could have gotten past the policemen. They could have snuck onto the towpath, but no way can they get past the river . . ." Thad sniffed and started again, "because the 'Aqueduct closed' sign . . ."

"Doesn't mention the trestle," Chris finished.

"And . . ." Thad pulled a small board out of his sleeping bag, "even if they got to the river, I took the trestle sign."

Mimi had sat down in the midst of them laughing, too, and even Partini, who almost never allowed himself the commonness of laughing, laughed. Jerry looked at the grinning misfits around him. Yes! He felt like shouting, but he just put on his shirt and laughed quietly too. For the first time in three days, he felt as if no one were looking over his shoulder. Watch out for us now, Bull, he thought.

Something about making it across the trestle with the sun bursting on his bare back, something about outwitting the cyclists and maybe even Bull Templeton, something about barreling down the towpath again as if they had slipped back into the tunnel—somewhere between time—made Jerry feel great. All right, he'd admit it, it felt almost as good as Vermont, like scrambling over the scree on Killington knowing you were getting close to the top. Ed Anderson seemed a long way off.

"Not too sweaty, Sebastian," Partini shouted as he bicycled up behind Jerry every so often, but even Partini had never pushed his shiny Peugeot so hard.

They sped past Lock 29 without a glance. No one even asked for water. They ignored the eyes of the gray stone lock-keeper's house. They streaked through minutes, past an overnight campground, past a field where cattle huddled under a single tree to escape the late afternoon sun, past an old bus half-buried in weeds.

But just past the bus Peter called out, "Something's wrong."

If it were a flat, that made number two for him in

one day. Jerry dragged his feet to a stop and turned. Peter looked sheepishly from his front wheel to Thad. "Sorry." He pulled his neck into his shoulders.

"Sorry," Thad repeated. Sometimes they were like the tall and fat of Tweedle-Dee and Tweedle-Dum.

Partini started at Peter mercilessly. "You cannot expect a small, frail machine to support five hundred pounds of blubber, Gollum. It is really that simple."

Zap.

Thad hopped off his bike and tripped over nothing at all as he hurried to Peter's bike. "Sorry," he said again. He put his nose to the frame, but not only was the tire flat, the chain was dangling on the ground, broken. "Not good," Thad muttered, his toss of red hair falling over his forehead as he fingered the end link.

"What?" Jerry stooped beside him.

"The link's broken." Thad shook his head like a surgeon disappointed in the outcome of an operation. "I don't have any extras."

Partini blew out one of his bagfuls of air. "How can you come so unprepared?" he said with as much disgust as he could muster, and he unstrapped his paniers. "I have to get away from this inefficiency, this incompetence, this . . ."

Chris had already set his bike against a tree and stretched out in a nearby field of green but already lacy Queen Annes, spread eagle, melting into the field like one more flower. Humming.

"Mimi, a short promenade perhaps, on the banks of the Potomac?" Partini invited as he locked his bike to a sapling.

When he got no response he turned to see her shaking her head no. She had already squatted next to Thad and Jerry. Partini went on alone, swinging his paniers and pushing the weeds away distastefully as he strode across the field. He dropped his paniers near Chris, and started off toward the woods, looking through the trees at something.

All four faces peered at the derailleur on Peter's bike, while Thad tried to bind the two pieces of chain together with his fingers. "The link is shot. I've got an extractor to take it out, but no replacement. I'm sorry."

Peter clutched his paper bag.

"What do we do?" Jerry said to Thad. When both had their fingers on the bikes, Jerry felt they were speaking the same language.

"We need a link," Thad paused, "and we don't have one."

"How about a link from my chain if it will fit," Mimi said. "My chain's got slack in it."

Jerry looked interested.

"We need a rivet. It's gone," Thad added.

Mimi took off her daisy button and pulled the spring pin out of the back of it. Then she sat cross-legged in the dirt next to the bike and carefully threaded the point through the rivet hole. It fit.

"Yeh." Thad grinned. "Yeh!"

Quickly, and yes, neatly, Thad extracted a link from Mimi's chain, relinked it, and attached the link to Peter's chain. Mimi fed in the pin, but she couldn't close it. Jerry, on the other side, fed his long fingers through the frame, and, taking the chain, bent the wire, by crimping it with his small pliers. Thad had stood up as if—wizard that he was—he needed to watch the entire operation from above. Jerry dropped the mended chain onto the derailleur and looked up at him, pleased.

"It's not perfect but it should work," Thad said.

"If you'll slip the tire, Jerry, I'll get the flat." Mimi brushed the dirt off her skirt and stood up.

"Oh, no, I'll get it." Peter apologetically rolled his eyes from side to side. "I can get it." He ran in a heavy trot across the towpath, set down his bag in the weeds and started back.

"No, no, we'll get it."

If they could just keep him out of the way. Jerry quickly unflipped the wing nuts, lifted the wheel out and rolled it to Mimi, who pried out the tire and tube. Then, lying on her stomach, her toes burrowed in the sand at the edge of the canal, she looked for bubbles from the submerged tube that would tell where the leak was. Peter sat back, the summer toad again, catching speckles of a late afternoon sun and clutching his brown paper bag.

They had only traveled about thirty-six miles today —way below their mark—with still over fifty to go to Washington. But by the time the bike was set upright in condition good enough to carry Peter to Seneca, the sun was slanting obliquely over the beech trees that lined the woods. Chris had fallen asleep in the field, and they discovered Partini had disappeared.

18

The name rang clear enough: "Sebastian!" It was Partini, but as the four of them turned to look across the field, they could see nothing. Just a patch of woods at the edge of the field. Mimi quickly dipped her hands in the water and, shaking them dry, rubbed them on her skirt and pulled her hair back behind her ears. "Let's go," she said. She couldn't have been over four feet ten.

Jerry slowly scanned the field and listened. But the voice didn't come again. Without saying anything more, the four of them pulled their bikes off the path, locked them around some young maples, then prodded Chris out of the field and started into the woods between them and the deserted bus. That seemed to be the direction of Partini's voice.

At the edge of the woods, Jerry stretched his arm out in front of the others, and listened again, but he heard nothing. Jerry motioned them toward the only thing in the field—the bus. As they crunched toward it, a wind blew the tether weeds all in one direction, making the bus look as if it were sinking in a brown sea. Thickly blue from a hand paint job, chips peeled in ribbons on the sides, and a crusted silver top bounced off waves of heat. A door hung outward, pulling on rusted hinges, and broken windows looked like eyes: asleep, awake, staring. A crooked sign read: SUNSHINE DAY CAMP. SOUTHERN CONFERENCE. The "SHI" was missing.

The bus looked lost, but as they approached the front, Jerry suddenly stopped. The others bunched up behind him. Something was moving inside the bus.

"Hey, Partini." Jerry tried to keep his voice natural. "Time to move out." He could hear the slight rustle of feet again, but nothing more. Peter, behind him, clutched his bag more tightly, the brown paper crackling noisily in the silence. Thad stood stark still.

A wind found a whiny passage through the opened bus windows. Jerry took a few steps closer, to a silvery tin can set on a makeshift rusted-grate fire that steamed just outside the bus door. Next to it, on a bus seat that belched a cloud of cotton stuffing, a bony, one-eyed gray cat lay stretched out, its yellow eye staring at Jerry.

"Partini," Jerry called again. "Hey, man, we're setting off." He could feel Mimi's hand lightly touching the back of his shirt.

But as he turned to whisper to the others, a face suddenly appeared at the door, a face with nearly no jaw, only whiskers that ran in a stubble down the no-chin and across a bony bird neck. Watery eyes peered out from under a kind of greasy train-conductor's hat. Thin fingers grasped a metal ticket punch dangling from a string. He was easily fifty years old, or seventy years old, or no age. Behind him, in the first seat, Jerry saw Partini slumped in a seat.

At first Jerry couldn't figure why the others were all cowering there like sticks. It was just an old man in a greasy hat. But then Jerry dropped his eyes to the man's knees. A torn-eared black mongrel crouched behind them, snarling, its lips curled up into a long, bristled nose. The phony conductor had nothing in his hands. No stick. No weapon. All he had was the dog, and it was clear that was all he needed.

"I'll ask again," he said and put his hands deep into the pockets of his frayed tweed jacket—its arms were short enough to reveal that he had no shirt beneath—"What do you want?"

Jerry looked quickly around him at the others. Thad was biting the inside of his cheek and shifting his weight from one foot to the other. Peter had puffed himself up and, crumpling his bag in one hand, stood closer to Jerry. Mimi simply looked back at Jerry when his eyes moved to her.

"Nothing . . . sir." He had a hunch the sir was what this fellow wanted. "Just our friend, and we're back on the towpath."

"The towpath is my front yard, sonny." The man moved his hand around in his pocket and pulled out a brown, dry wad of tobacco, broke off a part and tucked it into his already bulging cheek.

"Look, sir," Partini said from behind him. "We're just moving on. You've a lovely place here, but . . ." It didn't work with the conductor. His lips tightened into his nose almost like his dog's.

"That's my house, see?" He gestured back to the

bus. "My chairs. That's my stove. My friends visit me here. I am the judge and the police and the king . . . and the conductor of this place."

For no reason Thad bobbed his head and said, "Sorry," and the dog crept to the edge of the top step, lifted his upper lip and snarled.

"And you and your friends are illegal."

The man wasn't all there, probably a rail-rider who got too old to move on. And that dog with its runny eyes didn't look right either. Jerry watched the man finger the ticket punch.

"Listen," Jerry started cautiously. "We're just wanderers. We don't want to stop off here. We don't want anything."

"That's a lie." Watery eyes fastened on Mimi, moved down her face to her neck. "Him, back there, he was stealing out of my box."

Cripe, Partini.

"That's not altogether true, sir," Partini said behind him. "I didn't know anyone belonged to that box, those cans. I didn't know anyone belonged to this bus. God knows," Jerry could see Partini rubbing his nose, "I would never have taken a step in it."

In the late afternoon sun, the stench of the bus was probably enough to clear Partini's nasal passages for good.

Just then, Thad lost his balance and fell against the seat. The cat arched and spit at him, and the dog slid down the steps.

"Scratch!" the man shouted, and the dog slunk back behind his knees.

"Sorry," Thad said.

As the conductor stepped back in the bus, he blinked

at Jerry. "What kind of shirt you got there? What's it say?"

"It's a school we go to."

He laughed and Jerry realized he had no teeth; the tobacco was rolling around in a mouth full of gums. He probably wasn't as old as he seemed.

"School, ain't that nice. Well, now, you're attending my school. I am the—what you call it—the principal. That's it. Scratch there is the teacher. He's going to teach you something, see, and I'm going to get some friends who might want to see what I've caught in my own yard."

Mimi turned quickly, and for a moment Jerry thought she was going to make a break for it. Her eyes darted, but all around them was a wide empty field filled with last year's weeds. The conductor climbed out of the bus and came up behind her, and as he nudged her, she followed the others onto the bus. The dog snarled at each pair of legs as they passed him, his dusty black hackles raised along his back like a thick spine of bristles.

"You have a good class, Scratch. Teach them something," the conductor chuckled to himself as he loped away across the field.

Jerry stared at the dog which was staring at them. The one piece of advice his father had given him was to watch out for stray dogs.

19

No one spoke until they saw the conductor disappear around the corner of the towpath heading in the direction of the trestle.

"Well, Gollum," Partini whispered. The dog raised itself on two front legs.

"Well?" Peter answered, puzzled.

"Give him what's in your bag. Is it the beef? Bread? Whatever."

Peter clutched the bag to him. "There's no food in here."

Partini rolled his eyes up to his head. "This is no time to be selfish. Give something to him, fleshpot!" The dog snarled and pulled its lips back as it crept slowly forward.

"I can't believe this," Thad said, staring at the dog. His pink cheeks were pasty white.

Jerry slowly turned and looked toward the rear of the bus. In the very back, seats had been torn out and a mattress with gray ticking thrown into a corner. Bottles were strewn among the folds of a rumpled brown blanket. Down the center of the linoleum floor, a stream of something spilled into a dried brown pool.

"Sorry, I didn't have a hunch about this," Thad said. The dog lifted its head again at his deep voice, and Thad smiled. "Nice boy." He tried to settle back, but with his long legs, his knees buckled against the seat in front of him.

Peter spread himself sideways and whispered, "I could detain him while you all got out." They were whispering as if their words were traveling between them along a thin piece of string. "I know animals . . . I know dogs . . ."

"You could detain him with the food you have in that package, Gollum, if you weren't such a gluttonous slob," Partini hissed between his teeth. The dog sprang to its feet at the hiss and barked angrily at Partini, who pulled back into the seat.

The five of them waited again.

"Maybe if the door release still works, we could shut the door, lock the dog in, and get out the windows," Jerry suggested.

Mimi looked across the aisle to the small broken windows. "I don't think we'd all get out." Then she added, "Look, I'm not afraid of dogs. In the camp we live in summers there are always wild dogs, I could . . ."

"No," Jerry said. The dog raised its head at the change of voice, walked threateningly to the edge of the seats, pulled its lips back into a snarl, then slowly, paw by paw, let itself down there.

"Great," Partini whispered back. "Now the animal's almost in our lap." When Jerry didn't answer him, he said, "Well, what are we going to do for God's sake? Are we going to stay here? Are we going to wait for the conductor and his friends, whoever they are?" No one answered him. "Not me. There must be fifty years of putrification in this bus. Look at the floor. Clearly, urination." He stared up at the peeling ceiling. "I hope Templeton runs into a ninety-mile construction detour."

They were getting panicky.

"Wait," Jerry said and he nodded to Chris, who looked back at him quizzically. Chris had slumped in the third seat cradling his mandolin.

"The machine," Jerry whispered, gesturing at the mandolin.

Chris nodded. "Oh," he mouthed. Slowly, he brought his mandolin around in front of him as if it weren't even a motion. The dog had backed its way to the door, to the second step where the sun warmed the rubber strip. Chris started running his finger up a mandolin string making a thin whine. The dog lifted its scruffy head interestedly, cocked it. Then, as Chris went into a soft, wispy melody, the dog laid its head on the top step, its dark eyes watching Partini in the first seat.

Chris softly hummed one of his no-songs. The dog blinked, suddenly stood up and walked down the steps to the patch of sun in front of the door and yawned. Its yellow teeth drew sharp gasps of air as the melody seemed to wander over the strings. Even Jerry felt stretchy in the sun-heated bus, but he watched. They all watched.

Finally, the dog lay down its head. Only the yellow-eyed cat watched them without blinking from the bus seat outside the door. When Thad started to speak, Jerry shook his head, and after five minutes, Jerry, in

sign language, said he was going first. In stocking feet,
he placed one foot on the aisle floor and waited. Then
carefully he set his other foot down. A gold fly buzzed
across the fur on the dog's back and landed. The dog
shivered, and the fly darted away. Jerry took a third
step near the door and waited. On the fourth step, he
stretched himself over the dog's head to stand on a discarded piece of oil cloth next to the bus's seat where
the cat lay. The dog breathed deeply. Chris went on
humming.

Peter came next, heavily, holding his sneakers, his
thick legs cushioning him as he lifted and set down
each foot. Then Thad started away from his seat. Jerry
held his breath, watching the top of the bus door as
Thad moved toward it too quickly, but just as his forehead almost clunked it, Thad ducked and followed
Peter out the door. Finally, Peter, Thad, Partini, and
Jerry waited on the oil cloth as Mimi stood up.

It seemed that it would be easiest for her to get out,
but as she lowered herself out of the door, her skirt
caught on the ragged metal hinge, and she reeled backwards. Instantly, the ragged ear went up and the dog's
head lifted. Its runny eyes stared directly at her standing
in the doorway, but she froze—she didn't move a hair
—and the head slowly, slowly sagged heavily back to
the ground.

Still playing, Chris motioned them to go. Jerry shook
his head "no." Chris angrily nodded his head "yes,"
and he started into the aisle, humming as he stepped.
Jerry decided it was all right since Chris was coming
right behind them. After all, the sun was dropping lower
and lower. The conductor would certainly be back.
Perhaps he was coming now.

Jerry glanced quickly around them. They couldn't risk walking through the dry weed field, too noisy, but by stretching around the front of the bus, he discovered a low, marshy crevice that ran straight back from the bus to the woods next to the Potomac. That was the only way. He motioned the others to follow him.

Thad blinked at him, "yes," and Peter nodded. In a line, they edged around the bus toward the crevice, so close together they almost touched each other, until finally the wet, mushy earth swallowed the sound of their feet. There was just a quiet sucking sound as step by step they moved in their line. At a dip in the path, Thad attempted to put his right foot directly in front of his left, lost balance and teetered but he clutched Peter, solidly implanted in front of him. They started again. Mimi's feet barely left a footprint. Step by step they moved.

Jerry looked up at the woods only twenty feet or so in front of them as he placed each foot carefully. Slow motion again, but another kind. Fifteen feet to go. He looked behind to see Mimi staring down at the marshy path in front of her. Thad, a deep frown of concentration across his forehead, held himself together between Mimi and Peter. Ten feet. Ahead Jerry saw a mound of moss at the base of a huge sycamore tree, a quiet spot beyond the dry leaves. Five feet. Two. Finally he jumped into the soft, padded moss, then fell back against the tree. Thad landed in the moss next, Peter after him, breathing heavily, Partini, then Mimi.

But Chris was not behind them. Jerry's eyes followed the crevice back to the bus. Chris still stood silhouetted in the door. Jerry turned to the others.

"He'll make it." Thad said. "I'll concentrate."

Peter nodded.

"You do that, Wizard," Partini said, ready to break for it already.

"I think he'll be okay," Mimi said.

There really was little choice. "Let's go," Jerry whispered.

Tracing their way along a dirt line, they moved from the thicket to the angle of young maples that ran between the bus field and the field near their bikes. As they ducked in between the trees, Jerry caught a glimpse of Chris still at the bus door. Why wasn't he moving? Jerry shot another last look, then, quietly, started moving through the woods toward the bikes, shushing softly in the wet leaves. When they reached midfield, they ran, all five of them—in quick, short steps, long-legged leaps, hefty jogs—but they *moved*. Only Partini side-jogged to pick up his paniers. They headed for the bikes, dropped down to unlock them, then one by one, climbed on and coasted onto the towpath. Come on, Chris!

When there was no sight of him, Jerry motioned the others ahead, and coasted back along the path to the bus field. Chris was coming, all right, but not the soundless ditch way. He was running straight through the field, his mandolin flying in his right hand. Then Jerry saw the black slip of a tail sailing through the weeds behind Chris, first in a zigzag as he searched for a scent, then a straight line, heading directly for him.

Chris's hair flew behind him, and Jerry started to coast forward, his heart beating against his shirt. But he stopped short. Chris's bike was locked. Jerry coasted up to it, only to realize the lazy bum hadn't locked it after all. Thank God! Jerry picked the bike off the ground and, already rolling himself, handed it out as

Chris burst through the thicket. Behind him, the dog swept across the bushes in great leaps and barked wildly. Chris flung himself at the bike, the dog closer now, growling in angry gasps, biting at the air. As Chris threw his leg over the bar, the dog leaped at his leg. And got it. Chris dragged his leg—and the dog—pedaling as best he could with his other foot. The dog held on stubbornly, its head bumping into the derailleur as Chris, wobbling, slowly started to pick up speed.

"Scratch!" an old voice hollered. A figure had come hobbling onto the towpath with two other figures behind him. "Scratch!" it yelled. But the dog didn't let go. Its head lolling into the bike frame as if there were no neck bones, its feet only skimming the ground, it held fast. But Chris pedaled hard, his mandolin thunked against his back, and suddenly, he gave his leg a terrifying shake, and the dog ripped off a piece of his pants leg and rolled into a dust ball at the side of the path.

20

No way could they make Seneca before dark. But fortunately there was an overnight spot five miles up the road, with running faucets—and a long way from the blue bus. Even Partini had stopped asking for more luxury than that. A feast of dried beef, three boiled packets of lasagne and powdered milk drinks had acted like a sleeping potion. But Jerry couldn't sleep for long.

When he woke up the full moon had turned the field silver. Even the water faucet, tarnished in daylight, turned silvery under the glow of the moon. A slight wind tipped the feathery weeds which whispered in the field next to them. Jerry really couldn't sleep.

He pulled himself out of his sleeping bag, glanced at Thad, all six feet three of him curled, like Peter next to him, into a harmless ball. Not disturbing or bungling anything now. Partini, his neatly folded pants across his paniers, which he insisted on repacking every day, lay in his skivvies half in and half out of his sleeping bag.

Mimi lay next to him on a ground cover, her face like a round-cheeked China doll's under the open moon. As Jerry watched Peter, lying flat on his back now, his mouth opened and closed as he snored contentedly. That could have been what woke Jerry up. The mysterious bag was tucked half-open at Peter's head. Like Partini, Jerry had been certain it was full of food, but when they had put out their feast, Peter had tucked the bag behind him. Old Gollum was the tough one to fit in, bowing and scraping, and breaking screws and links and tires at a record clip.

Jerry looked one more time at the bag, then took in a deep breath of the night air and started across the silver field. At least they were here, together, a broken trestle away from the yellow cycle and miles away from the conductor. He felt strangely relieved tonight. His feet kneaded the soft earth, his toes sinking quietly into the cold mud beneath the weeds. No path here, really, but the river had to be ahead. Ever since he had been a little kid, he had looked for moments to go off alone. On trips, his mother would pull out her "plan for the day," and he'd slip off. "You keep getting lost," his mother would moan. But Jerry knew he never was.

At the edge of the field he looked toward the gray back flap of night sky beyond the trees. He could hear the river, lapping and coiling around the rock pockets on the shore. Like a maze, the trees stood quiet and still, lit by the night. A spread of rocks rose to one side, and Jerry walked out on them, curling his feet comfortably as waves crawled over the rock, touched his toes, then slunk away. Jerry climbed to the top of a dry boulder and sat looking at the river. In the center he could see an island where the trees had been bent by a storm. Last year's hurricane again. They were eerie silhouettes, stiff, leafy arms all pointing frantically in one direction: go, go. Across the river, a car's lights moved slowly from somewhere to somewhere. He didn't hear anyone step up behind him.

"Jerry."

He expected Chris but turned to see Mimi standing there instead. "I'm a light sleeper, even at home when my parents are there."

Jerry dropped his head in a kind of nod. Sometime during the day he had stopped being angry with her. He wasn't certain precisely why.

She sat beside him and, hugging her knees, laid her chin on one. "I wonder what the conductor would have done if we hadn't gotten away?"

"Taken us on a trip, that's what he told Partini."

"Some trip that would have been. How's Chris's leg?"

"Just a puncture. Peter took care of it."

There was a long pause and Jerry could see the wind blowing through the short hair around Mimi's face.

"Our bard got us out of a hot spot," he finally said.

Mimi put her head back. "Oh, no," she said. "Come on, come on, what's it all about, this bard stuff, this journey stuff?"

Jerry picked up a small stone and threw it toward the river. "Don't you know? Bards sing mysterious stories that get heroes out of tight spots."

"Oh, boy, that can't be true."

"Ah, but what's 'true'?" He smiled to himself. He had listened to that Morelli routine enough in the last four weeks. "Is what's true always real, or what's real true?"

She tilted her head at him. "Well, I never heard Chris tell one story. Or sing one."

Jerry shrugged. "He's a part-time bard."

She grinned and ran her fingers over the folds of her skirt. Her arms looked pale at night. "But you are trying to get to Washington?"

"That's what they tell me."

"It's a race against that other team?"

"A no-race race." For some reason he thought of Bull sitting in class, tipped in his chair by the window as if he were waiting for someone to prove something.

"But why? What do you get there?" She had sat back and was running the tip of her toe along the edge of a water pocket.

"Our hobbit English teacher says there's a ring there."

She grinned at him skeptically. "A ring."

He laughed a little. "Not a ring, a RING!" He struck his fist at the sky.

But she dropped her chin and looked up coyly at him. "All this for a ring . . . Woolworth's, maybe?"

And they started to laugh together until it wound down into a gentle shaking of the head. "It's just a game," Jerry said. And then for a moment night came up between them.

"I'm sorry I didn't keep my promise in Brunswick," she finally said.

"Brunswick wasn't all that terrific . . . we ran into friends; it was probably just as well you didn't try to leave from there."

Mimi dropped her hands into her lap. "Not the cyclists."

He nodded.

She stood up and looked at the river for a long moment, then turned.

"I can't believe it, they are crazy. Sixty miles from Indian Pool, for what? Did you talk to them, see them?"

"Well, we—"

But she didn't wait. "Look, there's more I should tell you about them—" she began, but Jerry wouldn't let her finish.

"Forget it, all right? They don't go on towpaths, remember?" He pulled her down as she passed and it occurred to him that her skin was as soft as it had looked when she was sleeping. "Particularly when the aqueduct is out and . . . the trestle sign mysteriously disappears."

She shook her head again slowly, staring at her wet toes. Thirteen. His sister's friend Mo Adams was thirteen and still pestered him like a nine-year-old when he played basketball.

"Look, who would have gotten us over the trestle if you had gone home?"

She grinned up at him, petulantly.

"And you did fix that tire in crack time."

"Remember I have an older brother," she started, then seemed to think better of it and stopped.

He thought of her grabbing that tire and taking it over to the canal without asking anyone anything. There was something about her. Her upper arm brushed his. It was plump like the rest of her, and soft.

It was something he would never admit to anyone, not even to his mother when she pumped him, but girls scared him a little. Even though he was nearly seventeen. Their eyes always looked into you. If they wanted to call you, they called you. If they wanted to meet you, they just cornered you someplace. Except for his sister, or Mo, who was more like a boy anyway, he never did know what to do with girls when they called or cornered him. But Mimi's arm felt good somehow. He would have liked to have told her that.

Pricks of light on the still river mystified him for a minute until he realized that they were reflections of the stars.

21

In the morning Thad and Peter spun out first. Peter's old Raleigh, the brown bag once again stuffed into the basket, looked as if it had new life, but at least with Peter biking ahead if there were any trouble with the chain everyone would know immediately. Chris, already humming, clanked after them. The ropes seemed to hold his bags less and less well. Jerry grinned as he listened to the noise. At first Partini waited for Mimi, his packing looking more like Chris's than usual, but when Mimi seemed to be hanging back, he pedaled off just as happily, in an almost upright position like an oldtime school teacher. Finally Mimi started off just ahead of Jerry who was riding "cleanup."

All right, Jerry had to admit it: he felt good about everybody. Even the towpath had turned friendly. It still felt like a tunnel, but a warm morning sun left leafy patterns on the path as it ran neck and neck with the canal. A frog belched a warm song in the shallows.

There wasn't any sand to struggle through, only hard-packed earth with a covering of leaves. For once he felt time was on their side. Templeton, look out!

"How you doing, Peter?" Jerry yelled ahead. He could see the broad back heaving from side to side.

"Good! Good!" Peter shouted back without turning.

The low whirr of Jerry's pedals sounded like the stubborn buzzing of an insect. As on the other days, in the quiet Jerry could almost see the canal barges from another time as he raced by. He watched Mimi's skirts flowing back from her bicycle seat. Like Peter and Partini, she had to love to eat; even her elbows were pudgy, but white and soft. There was no question she had to go home. Morelli would have their necks if they pulled up to the hostelry with her. If a sister of Jerry's had tried something like this . . . Push. Push. Her back moved evenly as she pumped her gearless Schwinn. Lord, the day felt good.

As they approached Lock 27, a broken lock with huge chips out of the concrete mouth and no doors left, the string of bikes slowed ahead of him, and Jerry looked up. Two young boys, fishing in the canal, waved.

"What are you catching?" Thad yelled.

"Goldfish," a boy in an Orioles baseball hat shouted back. Goldfish. Cripe. The canal was as tame as the towpath today.

Near noon a patch of sand slowed them slightly, and they swerved over to the harder grassy banks, but after a mile or so the path behaved again, and Jerry called a lunch break. He was getting used to taking charge. In fact, it wasn't bad at all. Three locks to go until Seneca. Jerry felt great.

*   *   *

"Not bad," he said out loud as he chained his bike to a tree and walked down a narrow path toward the Potomac. Everyone must feel great. Even Peter was struggling along. No flats. No screw trouble. Chain holding. Jerry lay down on the bank and took it all in. A motorboat racing along near the opposite shore, birds scolding each other. A gentle quiet. He listened. But then he listened more carefully. It was too quiet. Instantly, he sat up and found himself checking the trees. With Partini around, there just weren't chunks of silence like this. He turned the other way to see Peter and Thad, standing on the bank like two navigators on the bow of a ship. The brown paper bag lay at Peter's feet.

"Partini!" Jerry called suddenly. A suspicion nipped at him. He stood up. "Partini!" But when he stepped around a picnic table, two figures brushed past him. Partini and Chris were sneaking through the trees toward Peter. At the shore they pushed Thad aside, each grabbed one of Peter's arms and started to escort him into the river.

"Come on, Gollum! For two flats, a faulty screw, a weak chain and not using your lunch to bail us out of the conductor's hotel, a bath in the Potomac!" Partini announced as if to the world. He tugged one arm; Chris pulled the other, perhaps not wholeheartedly. But Peter just turned around. At first, he simply stared at them with his round, dark eyes, but then he stuck out his chin and slowly seemed to blow himself up with air; his Lockewood tee shirt expanded before their eyes. Suddenly, he looked immovable.

Partini broke to his rear and began to push. Chris pulled in front of him, but his feet slipped in place when the thick body would not budge. Finally, Peter simply sat down while the two of them wedged their feet against a rock and tried to pull him up, but they couldn't budge him. "Way to hold out," Jerry said, laughing. Peter was strong. They had not thought of that. Neither had Jerry.

But Partini was too hyper to give up without any success. Suddenly, he dropped Peter's arm and scooped up the brown paper bag and ran into the woods with it.

Peter rolled over on his side and, snorting, struggled to his feet.

"Watch me, Gollum dear, I am about to devour your goodies," Partini yelled through the trees.

Before Peter could get to him, Partini plunged his hand into the bag, but more quickly, pulled it out.

"My God." Partini closed the bag.

"It's hurt," Peter said. "Give it to me." His nostrils flared wide now, and his face was angrier than Jerry could have thought possible. Partini handed the bag back. "All right, all right." And Peter reached into the bag and slowly and carefully pulled out a good-sized hard-backed box turtle, its dark brown shell cracked across the upper half. Peter set it gently on the paper bag, and Jerry dropped to his knees for a closer look. The turtle had pulled into its shell, even the tail wound tightly under it, but the shell oozed flesh at the crack. The others circled the turtle, and Peter put his hand out as if to defend it from something. Or someone.

"If I had left it yesterday near Brunswick—, an animal would have gotten it, smelled the flesh . . ."

Partini wrinkled his nose at the word. Mimi tried to touch the turtle's head, but the turtle withdrew farther until only the two nostrils could be seen in the puckered folds.

"The shell will never mend," Peter went on, "but once the flesh heals, other animals will leave it alone . . ."

Partini turned his head as if from something rotting. "It isn't enough we have to get through Mirkwood, be half starved, escape mad dogs, we have to carry a putrifying turtle. Spare me the SPCA report."

Zap.

But Peter didn't smile. He didn't say anything either, but for the first time, he didn't smile.

Since no one had moved, the turtle slowly pushed its head out of the neck folds of dry brown skin: the nose first, then great wondering eyes. Finally, it stretched out, searching the air and blinking. Then, slowly, the stocky legs came out—one at a time—like children wondering if it were safe. Peter reached down and rubbed the top of the shiny head with his fingertip, and the turtle stretched its neck even farther like a contented dog getting scratched in a patch of sun.

"Well?" Partini finally said with his usual edge of impatience.

"I can't leave him, the raccoons, woodchucks, would—"

"Look, Gollum," Partini interrupted, "if you think you are nature's gift to the animal world, that is your murky view."

Jerry could feel the air bristle. "Ah, Partini," he interrupted, "why don't you get the lunch."

Partini left Peter and the others standing in a circle around the turtle who was slowly beginning to scrape across the paper bag, and, shaking his head, found his way back toward the bikes.

"Hey!" he suddenly yelled out. "The lunches are gone."

They all got up and walked back toward him. "What do you mean?" Jerry asked.

"They're gone. Disappeared. Kaput! I had the lunches in my left panier with my comb and shaving lotion, in a perfectly good plastic bag, and there is nothing there now."

The four of them looked at each other. "The conductor?" Thad asked.

"He must have stolen them," Partini filled in.

"Are you sure they aren't in your pack, Partini," Jerry asked.

"I'm sure. I'm sure." He tossed all the contents out of his paniers article by article. Brushes, scarves, towels. "I'm sure."

No one commented. Jerry simply went to his paniers and drew out their dinner food. Beef Jerky, coconut, sesame seeds and crackers. Thad pulled out some dried milk and Chris some raisins. They would just have to split the food one more way a day early.

The sun streamed boldly across the rocks after they ate. Everything seemed to settle down. Thad washed his pans in the river, stepping carefully until he stumbled over something on the bottom, then he dropped a pan. Retrieving it, he dropped two others that he had tucked under his arms. "Where's that pot," he muttered to the river. "There it is, no, there it is." Peter had blocked off an area in a marshy pool by the river to let the turtle laze in the sunlit shallows. Mimi leaned against Peter's back with Partini sitting in front of her while she braided his curly black hair into tiny braids. Chris hummed the song he had made up for Jerry on the third night, but he had added an almost banjolike strum. Jerry dangled his feet in the pond. He had a sudden wish Mimi were braiding his hair. Chris stopped strumming and whispered to him, "How could the conductor have taken the food?"

Jerry looked **up** at him.

"Remember? Partini's paniers were in the field with me."

22

The tires bounced over the towpath until Jerry's rear end felt as if it were being dragged down an assembly line of scattered bolts. Like a sleeping lion, the path had turned wild again after lunch from something they hadn't figured. With only twelve miles to Seneca where they could get a permanent rivet for Peter's bike and really begin to make time, they started into a stretch that had not been touched since the hurricane the year before. The hard-packed base of the original trail had been swept away, and storm-washed roots snaked across the path like gnarled fingers.

It was the worst thing for Peter's bike. In the next two miles, he dropped behind Chris, then Partini, and, finally, Mimi. Each turn of his pedals threw him into a new barrage of roots. Then four miles into the rough, the towpath was washed out completely. As the five of them drew up to a wooden barricade, they looked across a thirty-foot gap. The hurricane again. It had raked a river right through the path.

"This is precisely why I prefer traveling by air," Partini said, adjusting an imaginary tie. "First class, baggage carriers, stewardesses with magazines."

The difficulty only started with Partini. Crossing the stream, everyone helped everyone—it was narrow enough—but when Partini said, "Come on, Gollum, el drag-o, you'll need all the help you can get," Peter pulled his bike away and started down the hill at such a clip, that the soil gave way. He and the bike tumbled wheel over leg over wheel to the bottom of the gully. When he shook his bike upright on the other side, the pin that had been holding the broken chain together was gone, and the chain lay in two parts again. Peter sat down in a dusty heap staring at the chain.

Jerry let out a sigh. "I'll ride ahead to Seneca," he said. At least this time there was nothing to avoid in a town.

"No, I'll go." Thad's lips were set, and he started to roll out.

But Jerry caught his handlebars. "You stay with Peter and the others." The truth was, Jerry trusted himself most.

"You sure?" Chris asked.

"I'm sure," Jerry said. He tried to catch Mimi's eye but she had sat down next to Partini. "Mimi," he suddenly said. She looked up and started to lean toward him.

"Oh, nothing," he said, putting all his weight on one of the pedals. "Nothing."

*   *   *

Two bird-watchers stepped out in front of him on a turn. "It's a red-tipped pileated woodpecker. There!" a woman in riding breeches whispered.

An older man crowded into her binoculars. "No! Where? Lucy, where?" he pleaded as Jerry swerved around them.

Jerry's face dripped sweat over his headband, but he had already ridden six miles alone. The hikers were surely a sign that he was close to town. The towpath had changed, too. It had been freshly sanded here and packed down by hikers, probably hiking out of Seneca. If he could see the town around the next bend, that would be all right with him.

It is strange how a person can see something and not see it. He was staring that way, mindlessly, when he noticed among the heel marks, diamondback rattle-snake tire marks running down the towpath. Then he realized that he didn't know for how long he had seen them. His mouth suddenly felt dry. They were over-lapping marks from a tire bigger than a normal bicycle. Maybe a thick three-wheeler. Maybe some kind of cart . . . maybe a motorcycle.

Then he realized there could be more than two sets of tire marks. His eyes didn't leave them. They couldn't. Were there two cycles then? Three? Had they gone ahead of him or were they behind him? Where had they come from, for God's sake? The blood pounded behind his eyes.

Stupid, he suddenly thought. The cycles could easily have ridden ahead to Seneca by highway, then doubled back on the towpath! Suddenly, he wanted to see hikers, bird-watchers. People. He sat up straight, peering into the woods which seemed to rush at him from both sides. When he caught sight of a boy and his father lugging a picnic basket and two fishing poles off the path, he felt relieved. More than relieved. It was broad daylight, after all. But the tire marks didn't go away, and he left the boy and father behind and rode into another empty stretch.

A sign saying SENECA STONE QUARRY suddenly appeared in the clearing in front of him. Ten minutes earlier he would have been delighted; Seneca had to be just ahead. Yesterday, he was convinced no one knew they were on the towpath; he had wanted to keep it that way. That meant: stay away from towns. But if you didn't want to be trapped alone in the tunnel, other people were the only answer. He wanted to be in Seneca now.

His head began to reel from side to side. He spun to one side to search a rubble of rock, to the other to search a noise by the canal, back again when he heard something move in a deep swamp thicket.

The back of his knees dripped sweat. He pedaled into a curve, suddenly slowing his pace as one does when walking into an unlit room, but as he turned the corner and picked up speed the towpath tunneled again, into still another straight and empty corridor of trees. For a moment, the tire marks disappeared. Jerry jerked his head to the right, to the left, but saw nothing. The same old canal, the same old trees.

He regripped the handlebars and pushed the pedals down and down. "Where are you, for God's sake?" he suddenly shouted. "Get it over with!" No, that was stupid. He was doing a job on himself. Tire marks weren't tires. Push. He pushed his mind away from the tracks to Templeton, riding right into that ninety-mile construction site. To Morelli, grinning when he turned the van out of the empty lot. To Mimi, her arm warm against his arm last night. He pushed and pushed, a single bead of sweat winding down his back.

Then a roar burst on him, like an amplifier suddenly blasted on, and it sped out of the bushes at him: a black Kawasaki. Jerry gasped but gripped the handlebars harder and stared ahead. Where are the kids and fathers now? he wanted to shout. Where are the hikers? But then a second cycle turned at him from the woods ahead, another black metal shark sliding onto the towpath. It skidded the sand into the air as it sped past Jerry's bike and barreled around behind him. Jerry's ears burned. Then a third roar came at him from a field beyond the woods: a familiar sound. It was the yellow cycle, the yellow metal belly clutched by two black legs and the visored helmet-face turning the grips like faucets, squeezing him farther and farther onto the raised border between towpath and canal. Then, as suddenly as they had come, the cycles sped away down the path.

Jerry kept pedaling toward Seneca. That was his answer. He would keep pedaling.

For moments it was quiet. He was alone once more in the empty tunnel, but the roar came again, the growing sound of motorcycles gunning down the path toward him. Ready or not.

First one black metallic shark came, turning around Jerry's back wheel so close it clipped it, then swerving to the other side, forcing Jerry over toward the edge of the canal. Then before he could regain balance, the other black cycle spun around him from the left, revving its motor angrily and churning the path into dust. Jerry swerved instinctively, but the yellow cycle pressed him on the right, and as Jerry turned his head wildly, the black sharks streamed around on his left.

Suddenly, the swept bar of one of the cycles seemed to reach out deliberately to hook his own handlebar. It only brushed it. Breathless, heart pounding, Jerry tried to steady himself, but his tire mired in sand. The yellow cycle skidded into the same patch, throwing sand into Jerry's eyes. He reached for his eyes. His front tire wheeled, and as the rear tire stopped, the whole bike spun and crashed over him, inches from the canal.

There was quiet now. Jerry lay there, moving his fingers slowly across the dirt toward his stinging eyes, when he made out two black cowboy boots standing at his elbow.

"You alone?" a deep angry voice said to him. Jerry tried to look up through the painful blur.

"I said, you alone?" the voice said again, threatening.

"I'm alone, I'm alone," Jerry squeezed out. How would they know any differently? But the answer seemed to infuriate the voice. A boot suddenly stepped on Jerry's hand, the leather heel biting into his skin. Then, after twisting into his fingers, the boot moved to step on the spokes of his bike. All at once, it stopped. There were voices coming around the bend.

"Hazel, Hazel. Here."

Quickly, the cyclists remounted, and as one of the Kawasakis rolled past Jerry, the rider reached out and pulled the brake wires out on Jerry's bike, then kicked his cycle into a thunderous start. The others followed in his dust. Jerry was still rubbing his eyes when the sounds disappeared down the trail, like stones dropped into a deep well.

He turned and stared at the patch of sand. He had been wrong earlier. It was a mean little tunnel, and something else: sometimes alone wasn't so hot.

The bird-watchers came around the corner at a lazy clip just as Jerry shook his bike upright.

"You couldn't have heard anything, Hazel. There's nothing here but the swamps. That's why they nest here." Her binoculars bounced around her neck. "And it's so peaceful. No cars to fume them out of their nests. No noises to frighten them. Look, Hazel, look now." She set her feet apart like a conquering general's, and aimed her glasses at a singular tall tree towering above the lily pads where a brownish bird with red on its head had settled itself.

The gray-haired lady with a walking stick shook her head in awe. "It's amazing, Mary. What a peaceful spot."

23

Slowly, Jerry pedaled back to the others.

If he had not let his mind wander, if he had pedaled harder, not looked around, not let them throw him, maybe he could at least have made them run him into Seneca. He had let up. Cripe. The one broken wheel spoke was easily lifted out, the others weren't too badly bent, and it didn't really affect the wheel, though the bike rode with a slight weave. He glanced at his hand where a nail in the boot had ground into his flesh. It had stopped bleeding, and the blood had dried into a brown, clotted line. If only he had not let up. Lock 25. Goose Creek Lock. He could have gone on to Seneca alone, but somehow in the clutter of thoughts, he didn't want to be alone. Now, he pedaled slowly, finding his grip weak.

When he finally arrived at the washout, the others were nowhere in sight. Then he heard them down by the Potomac, laughing. He couldn't believe it. They were all stripped and swimming in the muddy shallows of the river as if nothing had happened. Peter sat like an immense beached whale in the marshes, the water lapping around his tremendous white stomach, the turtle on a sunny rock next to him. Partini swam after Mimi trying to reach a peninsula. Chris, naked as a jay, sat strumming on the end of the peninsula. Only Thad saw him ride up.

"Jerry!" he shouted, stumbling through the thicket to meet him.

"Hey!" Partini called out. "It's bath time. Bring your Palmolive and jump in."

Jerry dropped his bike by the side of the path and walked through the woods.

"What happened?" Thad tried to keep up behind him, pushing the branches that flipped at him aside. "What happened?" Then he caught sight of Jerry's hand where the blood had dried between his fingers.

"What happened?" Jerry answered. "The world has blown up into a thousand motors while you all were taking a bath. That's what happened." His words were tumbling over each other but he didn't care.

Peter had already rolled over onto his feet and run to get his towel. Hopping clumsily into his jeans, he reached for his antiseptic with his other hand. Jerry had become a wounded turtle. Chris set his hat back on, slipped into his jeans, and ran toward Jerry. Partini couldn't understand the activity. Finally, he waded in to shore, too.

"Incredible, Sebastian. You have a way of blowing even bath hour with your ponderous, Byronic pout!" He didn't hold back this time. "Sometimes I think you think you're Jesus Christ, for God's sake. Everyone running around like crack-brained squirrels. Look at Gollum. The ground is shaking." He pulled on his shirt. "Can't you handle things quietly by yourself? We elected you our hero, didn't we? What kind of a hero are you anyway?"

Then he noticed the hand as Mimi came up behind Jerry in a towel and took it.

"Look," Jerry pulled his hand away. "I'm no hero. I told you that. You either, Partini. Maybe none of us is. Let's face that." But he suddenly stopped and sat down. "Let's forget that crap. They're back. On the towpath."

"The cycles?" Thad said slowly.

Jerry nodded, taking the antiseptic from Peter and dripping some on the wound.

"Where?" Chris asked. He was unusually pale as he pushed his hat back.

"Ten miles up, maybe closer by now."

Partini sat down on the bench behind Thad. "They coming here?" he asked.

"I don't know."

"Well, you have to know. Did it look like they were coming here?"

"I don't know!"

Mimi sat down, her hair falling to either side of her face. "Look, I'm leaving, Jerry. Partini . . . Thad . . . I'm beginning to think it's my fault . . . no . . . I know it is."

Partini looked angrily at Jerry. "What do you mean? Sebastian gets his derriere hung up with motorcyclists every ten miles and . . ."

"Don't you understand, Partini, I know them."

"So?"

She sat down as if there were words bursting in her, but she didn't know which ones to let out.

"He's your brother, isn't he?" Jerry said at last, not sure he wanted to hear the answer.

Mimi sat back onto the stump and let her hands fall into the skirt between her knees. "Is that what you thought?" She smiled hopelessly and shook her head. "No, not that bad. The yellow cyclist, Bart Smith, is my brother's friend."

"What?" Partini broke in.

"My brother has taken off on his cycle, west, to Montana, Oregon, without telling my ma and dad. He told Smithy to keep an eye on me. And Smithy is pushy. Crazy. But I never figured . . ."

"Hey, but that's the answer," Jerry suddenly said. "He's . . . don't you see? He's got a little power, a big yellow machine, and he's crazy with it. The first time he ran us off, we didn't even know you!"

"But he never would have followed—"

"Wrong! He doesn't need an excuse, don't you see? When he's on that cycle he's against the world; we just happen to be in it."

Mimi seemed to listen for a minute, then she sighed deeply and stood up, but Partini pulled her down again. "I hate bad scripts. You're not going to leave now and turn this into B-movie stuff. No class. They're not coming anyway. Listen. Do you hear motorcycles?"

Jerry stared at Partini. "Hear them or not, Partini, they're there. And there's no way out of here except past them."

139

24

"Got any hunches?" Jerry asked Thad. The wizard had insisted on setting out first, but he shook his head.

"Sorry," he said. He wasn't smiling. He humped his lanky body over the small white bike and started his even pedaling down the path—all grace on a bike. It wouldn't be easy being first now, no matter how tame the towpath looked. No matter that two old gentlemen in hiking suits were ambling along, with a noisy family of five not far behind them. The chances were that somewhere on that path behind a lock house, in the woods, somewhere, three shadows were waiting.

After Thad had disappeared around the first curve, Partini and Chris started off. Partini had changed into a purple tee shirt with an iridescent rainbow sweeping from armpit to armpit.

"Keep humming, eh, buddy," Jerry called after Chris.

Chris grinned and clanked down the towpath. When

the two of them turned the bend, Jerry motioned Peter and Mimi onto the path. Mimi had lent one more link to Peter and the paper clip Jerry had found to hold it couldn't last long but it had to do. Jerry wheeled onto the path last, cleanup. The pattern was deliberate. A single biker would go first to flush anyone out, then the next two as warning, then the last three. They would ride separately, but within shouting distance.

Their pace was good at first. They only saw each other on distant turns, and there didn't seem to be any sign of anything unusual. But then they stretched farther and farther apart.

"Chris!" Jerry shouted, but there was no answer and Jerry could feel himself growing edgy. Every clump of trees that seemed to cling together too tightly, he searched for any color besides brown. Any movement.

At Lock 25, he felt his insides sink as the door to the lock-keeper's house swung open. Swinging doors can have an ominous look when you're waiting for something but don't know exactly what or where. When he heard motors roar from the woods by an overnight camp, his foot froze on the pedal, until he realized it was only two motorboats on the Potomac, throwing up a noisy wake.

Seven miles into the path he sighted the tracks from his earlier trip, and when he rode over the place where his bike had crashed, he shuddered. The place had a feeling all its own, a weird feeling. He felt certain if he ever rode past the place again, the feeling would still be in that spot, in those weeds, somewhere in the sand.

"I see the tracks," Peter called out. "I can see them." Poor Gollum. Of all the people to be stuck in a group that had to face anything, he would be the most useless. A good nurse, but useless blubber. Mimi? He just hoped she had enough sense to stay out of the way.

The clock in him started to tick again as he realized that they had ridden seven, eight, nine miles into their ride. Funny, he hadn't thought of Washington or Templeton since the cyclists had reappeared. It just wasn't the point now. Clouds had started to hang over the path again, heavy ones with thick arms that seemed to quarrel with each other in the sky. The path grew dark again, the canal a black, still stream. But Seneca couldn't be more than a mile away. One mile!

"Chris!" He shouted, but there was still no answer.

A half mile farther, a slight wind began to pick up, scooping twig leaves on the path and sending them in circles in front of the bikers, but they maintained their pace. At each bend now Jerry kept expecting to see the Seneca aqueduct stretch out in front of them. They might actually make it. If they did, he wanted the aqueduct to be the Roman kind. Something victorious. Something back in time.

A soft misty rain started to fall, carried by a light wind. Jerry's back felt cool. He saw Mimi wriggle her shoulders comfortably as the mist gathered on her neck. He had never liked plump girls before, but Mimi just couldn't be any other way and be Mimi. All that pizazz. The rain started to catch on his glasses and gather in the rims, and the wind started to pick up, but his clock told him Seneca had to be around the next bend. It didn't matter now that the others had ridden too far ahead.

But the wind blew into the tunnel in cool circles. The path grew darker, and at the bend where Jerry expected the aqueduct, a rumbling sound suddenly rolled out at them from a picnic area. Jerry recognized it all too soon. It was the cyclists. But this time they didn't run circles around him. They had simply and silently let the other three go by and now they stood straddling their motorcycles across the middle of the towpath as Mimi, Peter and Jerry rode toward them. There was no point in shouting.

Jerry looked at the three black one-eyes and the white-toothed grins. His heart pounded in his ears. Ideas crashed in his head. Take Mimi's hand and run. No, pretend to talk to them, pass time, until the family of five catch up . . . no, stay on his bike, and when they get off their cycles, push off again. Or yell; maybe Partini and Chris were bicycling back. The ideas exploded one after another without any one coming into focus.

Poor Gollum, Jerry suddenly thought. Pale and blank, he had pulled up and just stood there, facing them, his jaw shut tight and his huge toad chest swelled out. Lord, he was big. The three cyclists, still on their bikes, grinned at him and prodded their wheels into his as one would prod a strange trapped animal to see if it were dangerous. It jarred the paper bag still stuffed in the basket and Peter backed up a little. The middle cyclist prodded Peter's bike again. Peter backed up again. He was going to buckle, Jerry knew it. They didn't know that Peter was two hundred pounds of bluff but they would any moment. The cyclist laughed as he let his machine glide into Peter again and again. Finally it tipped his bike over. Flat-footed and grunting, Peter scrambled to catch it and the bag at the same time.

The cyclists laughed at the fumbling Gollum. They knew Peter was nothing but air. Having determined that, the yellow cycle backed up, passed by Mimi and glided toward Jerry. Good, Jerry thought, leave her alone. When the cyclist came to Jerry he just stared at him. Hard to believe the helmet had a name. Smithy.

But something happened as Jerry stared back. He realized that as long as the cyclists were on their metal monsters, they weren't equal.

"Why don't you get off that thing?" Jerry taunted. "Is it tied to your balls?"

The one-eye said nothing. At first he gave the cycle another nudge into Jerry's and another and another. But Jerry didn't back up. "Come on, get off that monster. That piece of tinfoil." As he taunted, the other two slid their black Kawasakis around and eased them back, ignoring Peter and Mimi.

Jerry felt the front tire of the yellow cycle rub against his knee. It sent a chill up him and his mouth felt like dry paper. He found himself licking his lips, swallowing for moisture.

"Come on, you yellow bastard," Jerry urged. One of the other cyclists coasted up alongside the yellow machine and pushed his machine sideways into Jerry's derailleur. Suddenly, Jerry's hand throbbed. If only Mimi and Peter would take off.

"Just chicken shit on a cheap motorcycle," Jerry taunted. "Chick, chick . . . chick."

"I don't hear so good," the cyclist on the yellow machine said.

"Oh, but you do, big shot. I said chicken shit."

The cyclist sat back on the riding seat of his motorcycle and leaned forward.

"Forget it, Smithy," one of the other cyclists said.

"How can you forget a chicken like that?" Jerry persisted.

"Smithy!" Mimi called, but he didn't even turn. "Smithy!"

Slowly he threw his leg over the seat and jammed down the kickstand with his boot heel. He threw his black helmet next to his cycle without taking his eyes off Jerry. If only Mimi would take off. Jerry warily got off his bike, still pinned between the front tires of the two Kawasakis. But he could see the face of the yellow cyclist for the first time and it startled him. He was twenty maybe, narrow nose, thin tight lips that went with that light mustache. Smithy. Something peculiar about knowing that.

Jerry swayed from his hips, waiting. But where did you throw the first punch when you were playing someone else's game? His neck throbbed. Where did you throw it when you could see the narrow nose and thin lips? When it had a name: Smithy? But one of the other black cycles shoved him again, and from the rear something hammered into his back. Jerry spun around to see a black helmet leering at him. Then a hand hit him in the chest and he fell back. He grabbed a tree to keep himself from stumbling, losing himself, but another hand grabbed his shoulder and twisted him around, and without thinking, Jerry threw his fist into the leering face. The cyclist staggered back.

"Get out of here!" Jerry yelled to Mimi and Peter. But suddenly, he heard a wailing groan.

The cyclist in back of him had doubled over, pulling his helmet off as he groaned. Peter had put his great arms around him and was squeezing the air out of him.

An angry bear. The other two cyclists ran over to the bear, whose face was red with sweat, his neck bulging angrily into his shoulders. The one with the visor still on tried to break Peter's grip, but Gollum's massive arms belted his companion like an iron vise. He squeezed again, and the trapped cyclist grunted helplessly. "Ahhhhhhhh," he moaned.

Now the yellow cyclist careened into Peter's back with his shoulder. Peter bellowed but didn't let go, and Jerry came around and dived at the yellow cyclist as he recovered, pulling him into the woods. The two embraced in chest grips, finally rolling into the trunk of a tree.

Peter turned, still clasping his captive, and lifted him into the air, then set him down, lifted him then set him down. Harder and harder. The cyclist's face looked as if the blood had been squeezed into his head. The one free cyclist sliced his knuckles into Peter's back.

Jerry twisted over onto the towpath trying to get to Peter just as Mimi rolled her bike out and started pedaling down the path. When the helmeted cyclist saw her, he hesitated for a moment, looked at Smithy, and struggled to get away, but Jerry rammed his head into his stomach and he thudded back against the machine. Now the yellow cyclist ran toward his cycle. As he passed, Peter dropped his cyclist and swept around to grab Smithy, but he jammed his elbow into Peter's massive stomach. Peter fell back against his bike, staggering into the swampy grass as Smithy swung onto his cycle, jumped the starter, and shouted, "Ride."

Still holding his ribs, his lip bleeding, Jerry grabbed Smithy's arm, but the machine had caught on and rumbled threateningly. With Jerry still hanging on, the helmetless rider revved his yellow monster and rolled into a start that he blasted into speed. Jerry recoiled as the thick wheels skidded away in a storm of sand.

"Gollum!" Jerry turned to see Peter struggling to pull his bike out of the swampy field that dropped below the towpath bank here. Jerry waded down the bank, his feet sinking step by step into the tufted swamp weeds. When Peter pulled up on the handlebars, Jerry lifted the rear wheel, strung with weeds, out of the muck. Backing up the bank, they set the bike on the towpath. The bag was wet but intact. Peter squatted down and put his finger on the tenuously held chain. It hadn't held.

"They ran, Gollum. They ran," Jerry called exultantly. Jerry shot a quick look down the clouded towpath. "You walk the bike in, Peter. I'm going after them."

That was the thing about Ed Anderson. He tracked Jerry and tracked him, no matter how Jerry fooled him. Then one day Jerry turned the tables when he came for him. Jerry faced him and stood his ground. It had been messy and no winners, but poof, no more Ed Anderson.

25

Jerry didn't see a single face he knew, but he saw a hundred faces as he rode his bike onto the Seneca aqueduct. Kids with fishing rods lazed over the still sun-baked sandstone masonry, one holding a string with two miniscule fish. A stuffy type with a pipe, legs crossed, sat with his knees up, puffing and watching the river, while a determined group of men and women with binoculars crowded across the aqueduct squeezing Jerry to one side. It was happening again. The world had exploded and no one noticed.

Jerry coasted quickly off the aqueduct checking the faces, listening for motors. Seneca had been a real canal town, he could see, but it was more a tourist town now. He coasted past old frame buildings, a trailer hot-dog stand. He pedaled past a visitors' bathroom. He was back in the present all right: kids looking for "Gramps! Gramps!," a baby squealing at being forced into a stroller. Jerry tried to stare through the mass, but he couldn't see a single familiar face. Not a bicycle. Not a motorcycle. No plump gypsy in a yellow skirt.

Then from behind him, a tall voice bobbed over his shoulder. "Did you see them?" Thad asked. "What happened? Where's Peter?"

Jerry turned quickly and braked to a stop. "We saw them all right." Thad had his paniers in his arms and his strip of wrenches dangling against his side. Behind him, Partini and Chris climbed up a creek path toward them. Jerry caught sight of their bikes parked in front of a brown, weathered cabin-like building with a BICYCLES FOR RENT sign plastered across windows that could be propped up during the day. But Jerry kept on searching, scanning the building, the racks of bikes, the boats pulled up on the riverbank.

"She's gone," Thad said.

Jerry turned slowly. He needed to understand. "To call her parents?"

Thad shook his head and looked at Jerry from under his thick, almost white eyebrows like a great sad rabbit.

"What do you mean, she's gone?" Jerry turned to Chris for some kind of confirmation.

"She went with them," Chris said.

"That's impossible!" Jerry said.

Partini stopped the debate with his two hands. "When she came across the bridge, we were waiting, but the cycles roared up behind her, scattered everyone else, some running for the police, an old lady yelling 'no cyclists on the towpath.' Meanwhile, Mimi and the cyclists are having a shouting match—an embarrassing scene really—the cyclists coast down the road along the river and Mimi goes after them. Simple."

"She pretended she didn't know us," Thad added sadly. "When they started off, she went after them. No one made her."

"How do you know no one made her?" Jerry said.

Chris sat down with his mandolin against the V root of an oak tree. "It's true, Jerry old boy," he said.

Thad reset his wrenches over his shoulders and paced nervously toward the aqueduct and back, then toward it again.

"He's coming," Jerry said impatiently. "Gollum's all right. Those creeps won't forget him for a long time." Then he turned to Chris again. "She was pedaling after them? You saw her?"

Chris nodded. He had settled back and started to sing, " 'Poor boys,' said the wizard, 'they've . . .' "

"Knock it off, Chris," Jerry said. He couldn't understand his own feelings. Once when he had been forced to go to camp when he was ten he had had angry knots in his stomach for the first week. But when he had rolled his sleeping bag to go home and saw the other guys leave, he had felt a terrible loneliness. He hadn't wanted Mimi to hang on the way she had. But things had changed.

"I'm going after her," he said and rolled his bike out. "You can come or not."

"Hey, hero. You're not using your head!" Partini said and he grabbed the handlebar of Jerry's Peugeot.

Jerry tore it away from him. "Maybe that's okay." He coasted down the hill toward the sandy road, which turned into macadam.

"It's stupid, Sebastian!" Partini shouted. "If she's anyone's she's mine, but I'm no fool!"

"Wrong!" Jerry didn't turn back. He felt the macadam begin to smooth out under him. "She's nobody's."

"You're going to fight three machines over someone who *wants* to go?" Partini's voice trailed behind him. "It's stupid!"

Jerry didn't look up. Something swept him down the road like the wind, past the miniature town with its porch bungalows, trailers, and gas stations. He wanted to shout: Mimi, wait!

But he pedaled, churning each foot as if he were going to drive the pedals into the road. Whirr . . . whirr . . . whirr. He took a curve at a dead end at breakneck speed, his chin nearly touching the bars. A truck came up behind him as he raced onto a small highway that headed west to Brunswick, maybe thirty miles—backward. He didn't care. He just stared into the gray strip ahead. Woosh, another Tonka truck, brilliant green. He just wanted to see that old beat-up red Schwinn.

He drove his legs, spinning his Peugeot farther and farther down the highway. At a red light, he stopped. An endless red light, but he ached to race again when he heard the rattling behind him.

"Hey, man!" It was Chris, actually sweating, ringlets of sweat channeling down his cheeks and neck.

"We can't let her get sucked along with . . ."

". . . friends," Chris finished for him.

Jerry turned around and looked at him again as a Hertz Rent-a-Truck shifted noisily next to the two of them and ground on.

"Friends, Jerry. Not ours but maybe hers," Chris said.

"Forget it." Jerry flipped his pedal up.

"Come on, Jerry . . . want me to hum it?"

"Bug off, Chris." Jerry coasted into the intersection, but Chris coasted alongside him.

"This isn't your path, check it out, Jerry. It's going the wrong way."

"For you," Jerry snapped. He stepped on the pedal and broke ahead.

"No," Chris shouted. "For you, too, Jerry." He was keeping up, lapping Jerry's rear tire. "Washington's the other way!"

A chill ran down Jerry's neck. Ahead a wing of a TO ROUTE 112 sign was bent and just beyond it a four-mile construction sign was posted. Down the highway it was blue and nothing. Bull Templeton and the others could have ridden past this same light, this same spot, two hours, maybe three, maybe a day before. Going the other direction.

"She's really gone, isn't she?" Jerry suddenly shouted.

"So are the dragons, buddy," Chris shouted back.

Jerry pushed his hair off his face and turned his bike in a wide circle across the highway. "Okay, Chris," he said. "Go!" She'd be all right because she was Mimi.

26

Partini belched. "Let's get going!" he said.

Thad, coasting toward him, swallowed as if he were going to let the words out slowly enough to make perfect sense. "We can't. Just down the hill, the towpath turns into white chunks of concrete."

Peter followed, running his bike up behind Thad's, his toes pointed out, each foot landing heavily as he trotted. Only the ring around his thick neck was white, his face burned red. "It's true. Nearly a mile of towpath has been washed out," he panted, "and rebuilt with concrete chunks. They haven't put the sand on yet."

Jerry had been lying in the sun on the small green strip of grass between the canal and the towpath. Great! The hurricane again. He turned over and hit his head on the ground, realizing too late that something was beginning to throb that hadn't hurt when the fight was over. Partini had been gathering together his wrappers,

153

a towel-wrapped shaving kit and his deodorant. He stopped abruptly, leaned against a more-than-arm-sized oak tree and cocked his head skeptically at Thad. Chris sat up.

"We have to get off the towpath," Thad continued. "But it's the perfect time, see?" He unrolled the rolled map over his handlebars. "That hairline road north of the towpath going east is River Road. It connects with a small highway right into Washington. No trucks, no policemen, no . . ."

Jerry looked down the tunnel. The late afternoon sun threw angled shadows across it, giving it the appearance of a dozing lane, its eyes half closed.

"And with our being out of money . . . and food," Thad was saying. The Seneca bike shop had given them the rivet for their last 10 cents. Since they had eaten most of their last dinner at lunchtime thanks to the theft of Partini's lunches, two packets of raisins and coconut marked the end of their food.

"It's the only way out," Thad ended.

"No," Jerry heard himself say.

Thad stopped and stared at Jerry as if he hadn't heard correctly. "What do you mean, 'no.' "

"No. I don't feel like letting the towpath beat us."

Thad had gotten off his bike. "Jerry, it's a mess ahead."

"I don't care!"

"You're stubborn!"

"Maybe I am!"

Jerry lay with his chin on the ground while Thad packed up his map rolls under the bungi cords without looking at anyone. Then Thad turned around.

"For nearly two hundred miles I have followed you. Now I give one suggestion—well, one suggestion I really believe in—and you don't listen. I mean, isn't it possible I could know something?"

Jerry kept looking down the tunnel. It looked peaceful here, like a scene out of a garden magazine, but he knew Thad was right about it.

"You're turning your back on a clear road. Or maybe you just *like* to fight dragons!" Thad's voice was growing deeper and louder. "Maybe all of you do."

"They've gone, remember," Jerry said into his arm.

Thad backed his bike up so angrily, his rear tire caught the edge of the canal slope and nearly slid in. "Sorry," he said to it. Peter put his arm on Thad's shoulder, and Chris hiked himself up as if he might get into it too, but suddenly Partini started to laugh. He pushed himself away from the tree.

"I was right the first time," he said. "This is pathetic! How so much stupidity could be gathered onto so few blades of grass is beyond me. After nearly four days of a ridiculous amount of sweat, you still don't get the dragon thing, do you?" Partini had started to circle as he spoke. "None of you!"

Thad's chin dropped. "I get it."

"No, of course you don't get it, Wizard. Because if you got it, you wouldn't think we would ever find a really clear road. Not even when these four or five days of madness are over." Partini paced directly out of his circle toward Thad and whispered, "Dragons live on every road, Wizard," he turned to Jerry, "and every tunnel. And they don't all look alike."

Peter nodded behind him.

"Were the cyclists the only dragons?" Partini rolled on, "How about the conductor? The rivet that kept disappearing? The stolen lunches, the hurricane . . ."

"You, Partini?" Chris said without lifting his eyes.

"All right. Aren't we each other's dragons sometimes? They're on any road!"

"Cripe, Partini, then a dragon could be anything," Jerry said.

"Or any one, baby," Partini said.

Thad had started to hang his head. "So maybe we should all go our separate ways."

Partini dropped himself back against the tree, his puffed chinos gathered in a balloon around his waist. "Oh, that's a magnificent solution." He swept his arms upward. "After your fine speeches to me, it's everybody do what you want. Please yourself. Why do anything because the team said so? After all, what is a team anyway, just a package of smelly sneakers, broken animals and clumsy scarecrows with maps sticking out of their ears. I mean," and he climbed on the picnic bench and bellowed, "everybody for himself!"

That brought a staggering silence. A three-year-old running circles around the bench stopped, stared at Partini then broke for the safety of his parents' blanket.

"I'm sorry," Thad said.

"Enough of your sorry. There is nothing to be sorry about."

"Sorry," Thad said. Partini sat down in a breathless stare and left an empty space that no one else filled.

There was just a charged silence. And more silence.

Jerry stared at their faces and waited. Thad was right. Partini was right, but in spite of their speeches, the garbage still seemed to be Jerry's. But he had to take it out right this time and not alone.

He rose slowly to his feet. Even his knees ached. "Let's take a blind vote." He bent to search for some stones in the tufts of grass. "White, it's the road. Black, it's the towpath." The others bent over fingering the grass for stones, too. Chris rolled over on his side to reach some. Then they stood in a circle facing each other with their fists closed.

Jerry looked across at Partini, his hair in a thousand sweaty curls from his outburst, then to Thad, who turned away biting one edge of his lip. They were ready. Jerry turned his hand over and opened his fingers. Black. The towpath. He turned to Thad who, one at a time, opened his long fingers. White. The road. Then Partini. White. And Chris. Black! Jerry looked up at Peter, silently sweating on the opposite side of the circle. His four-day-old Lockewood Academy tee shirt was stained with heavy underarm perspiration circles. His fist was shut, his knuckles, white. He looked at Thad quickly, then slowly, he turned his fist over and opened his fingers. A tiny black pebble was caught in the fold of his thumb. The towpath.

As they swung their bikes onto the path, Partini muttered at Peter, "That's an intriguing vote, Gollum."

"I figure we are getting better at fighting towpath dragons." Peter smiled.

Partini shuddered. "Some of us are, Gollum. Some

of us never grow beyond the thousand-pound-bag-of-sand stage." He shot his foot down into his pedal. "And never will."

Jerry noticed Peter's neck bulge as he started off. Partini couldn't have heard what Jerry told them about the fight.

27

In the late afternoon sun, with the canal borders neatly clipped and a PLEASE DON'T THROW AS YOU GO: KEEP MARYLAND BEAUTIFUL sign posted, the towpath looked like a harmless park trail. If it were a dragon itself, it looked tame. No one was talking about Washington, but they all knew it couldn't be more than twenty-five miles away. Jerry threw a glance back at Peter. He had insisted stubbornly on riding cleanup this time, as if something were bothering him. As if he were trying to prove something. Not like Peter.

Jerry moved his pistons, taking advantage of the slightly wider towpath to pass Chris and Partini. Through the trees, Jerry could see a dam across the Potomac, intact, the water boiling neatly over a concrete strip. No sign of hurricane damage here, but then, just moments up the path, Thad jarred to a stop. "There it is," he said.

Jerry pulled up alongside of him, followed by Chris.

"It looks like the dumping ground for Mount Sinai's gallstones," Partini muttered riding up behind them.

Ahead of them, as far as the eye could see, lay a bed of white concrete chunks. A hiker walked up behind them and stared. "Man," he muttered and he turned back toward Seneca.

"Good old Hurricane," Partini clucked. "What do you say, O Great Leader? How does River Road look now?" His preppy beige pants had some grass stains on them, and he was getting the stubble of a beard.

"See, no side strip!" Thad said. "If we're going, it has to be across the concrete."

Jerry lifted his bike. "We can make it."

"Absolutely," Peter said, checking the turtle in its bag.

Partini filled his cheeks with air and let it out slowly. "Gollum . . . you know as much about rock roads as your turtle knows about Chinese cooking in a wok pan."

Zap.

Peter didn't smile but Partini didn't seem to notice.

Thad set out after Jerry across the endless white road of concrete which jarred the bike tires, jerking them from side to side. Partini started out next, at times picking his bike up and carrying it short distances by the center bar, then dropping it with an exhausted sigh. Chris crowded in next, then Peter. The stones bit at the undersides of Jerry's sneakers, as his ankles twisted into the shifting chunks. He tried carrying his Peugeot, too, but light or not, after ten yards or so, he dropped it. As he walked it over the rubble, each whack drummed against his elbows.

The concrete chunks just wouldn't end.

"Maybe this is what they mean by keeping Maryland beautiful," Partini muttered. Then he belched.

Thick trees bent over the towpath at this point, shielding the bikers from the heat of the late afternoon sun, but as the canal curved and widened in its rush toward Washington the pounding didn't stop. Only after nearly a quarter mile did the rubble disappear and the hard-packed earth path begin, neatly edged once more by grass. Again, it was as if the hurricane had never happened.

The four others laid their bikes down and sat on the lock side at Pennyfield lock and waited for Peter. He was having real trouble. With each step, his sneakers spread over rough chunks like melted plastic, and his cheeks blazed with heat.

When he finally pushed his old Raleigh up, Partini said, "I thought they only had goldfish inhabiting this canal. I forgot about the Great White Land Whale!" Peter didn't even look at Partini as he coasted out but Jerry could see his neck bulging angrily and Jerry put himself between Peter and Partini on the trail. He began to feel as if he were holding his thumb on a lighted stick of dynamite in a bottle.

Then they pulled up at washout number three. The five bikes rolled up to a wooden barrier at the edge of a jagged ravine that zagged from the Potomac through the towpath and canal into a junglelike underbrush of vines and trees. At the bottom a brown river churned through it.

"There's no way across," Thad said. "I mean, it's wide and . . ."

"Deep," Chris said peering over his handlebars at the swirling river that was almost pondlike in parts.

Jerry looked down the path they had just pedaled.

"Unless . . ." Thad said. Without finishing, he started climbing down the bank, but the sandy loam crumbled under his weight and he fell, sliding down the ravine as if his limbs were disconnected, tumbling over on his side and stopping inches from the fast brown stream.

"Well, spritely-footed Wizard, this bodes well for any crossing!" Partini called down to him.

Thad crawled to his feet, knocked off the chunks of mud and started along the shore of the river, finally passing around a corner out of sight.

Within minutes he shouted in his deepest voice, "I found it!"

Everyone but Partini strained to see. When Thad came around the corner he was carrying a long thin eight-foot plank, which he laid across the narrowest neck of the stream to an island clump four feet from the other edge. A person pushing a bike might make it across such a long thin plank—if there weren't too much weight.

"O Great White Whale, O Protuberant Toad, O Gollum, you are in trouble." Partini laughed. He was not letting up today.

Jerry went over the barrier to check the cliff and stream. The plan was simple. The five of them would go over the board two at a time, one pulling and steering the bike, the other pushing it. They would hand their bikes over the last four feet. Peter would push his bike over the plank last. They would know by then how much weight the board would carry.

Thad looked up worriedly at Peter. "I'll take the turtle," he said.

The little gully had a yellow look to it, the sandy

bank looked yellow, even the brownish river seemed to have a yellow tinge. The team started across one at a time. Chris and his bike went over easily, both bike and person only skin and bones. Jerry and his Peugeot and even Thad carrying Peter's brown bag on his light-weight had no problems; they went like birds picking their way across a limb. Jerry pulled for Partini, who bent the board so far it touched the water with each step, but seeing it, Jerry pulled the bike quickly, and Partini inched carefully, springing the board only slightly. Finally with a last bounce, he jumped to the island clump, then after Jerry lifted his bike across he jumped to the other bank, where his left foot slid into the spongy yellow mud. He could hardly pull his boot out.

"Aw Gawd . . ." he muttered. "A hundred bucks shot. You'll never make it, Gollum old boy."

Jerry watched Peter's neck, yet Partini was right. Where it was most shallow, the bottom was a silty, sucking sponge. In the middle and to the side, it was deep, and yet no way would the thin board hold Peter. Maybe in the vines, hidden, Jerry could find another stronger board, a limb, something.

Jerry had started into the brush, when he heard a grunt and turned to see Peter throw his paniers to the other side. Then he pulled his bike up onto his shoulders, adjusted it across his back, and waded into the murky stream.

"Come, come, Gollum," Partini taunted. "Let's not be dramatic." Peter's face blazed that sweaty red again as he struggled to set the tires at a steady angle to carry the unwieldy machine across the stream.

"It's too much," Jerry said. "Too deep in the middle,

Peter. Stop!" He tried to reach him, but Peter had started across. Everyone else drew to the opposite edge of the ravine above the river.

The quickly moving brown water swelled and passed around Peter's ankles as he inched slowly into the silty creek. As he moved farther into it, it swirled around his knees, pressing his jeans to his legs. He tottered, the bike slipped to the right, as his foot stumbled over or into something on the bottom. No one on the other bank said anything, not even Partini. There was just Peter's deep grunting. Bending over, slowly he adjusted the bike across his shoulders and pulled at his foot. The brown water churned as he felt for the next sucking step. And the next.

He had waded nearly to the middle of the creek. He was going to make it. Then, before their eyes, his foot seemed suddenly to sink so deep he dipped in up to his chest. His knee buckled and the front wheel swung over his shoulder. Reaching forward to catch himself, the other wheel fell backwards across his neck and pulled the frame into the creek.

Thrashing to grip the bike by the raised seat, Peter again looked like an angry bear. Water flew across his arms as they broke the current looking for the wheel or the center bar. Anything. He foraged helplessly trying to grasp something, at the same time searching for footing. Then, unexpectedly, Peter careened to the right, into center stream, and sank below the surface.

"I don't think he can swim," Thad whispered and dropped down the cliff with Jerry and Chris sliding after him, tumbling rocks and loose clumps of earth. A large brown circle spread out from a silent center.

Jerry waded into the shallow water by the board and

stared for a second. The circle had touched the shore. Not certain where to go, Jerry shoved the water aside, dipping into the deeper part. Then he saw a humped swell break the surface and send a new circle outward.

"There!" Chris shouted from the shore, and pointed, and Thad broke toward the circle, but suddenly ten feet away an elbow broke the surface. Jerry and Thad converged on the whirlpool it created, struggling themselves through the quicksand bottom. But they grabbed at nothing.

"There!" Chris shouted again. At a spot downstream nearer the shore, a huge dark head broke the surface, then a back swelled up, water cascading off its shoulders: Peter. He held a black frame, which he dragged alone to the other side, and up the cliff, stepping on the clods of earth he could find. At the top, he dropped the bike. The others pulled themselves to shore and up the cliff.

"Gollum, you are a mess!" Partini said to him. "Mud on your shirt. Look, your zipper's shot. Can't you keep yourself together?"

Peter looked up at Partini for a second, then grinned. "Partini," he said. "You're an asshole. But it's okay."

28

But Peter's bike wasn't okay. Old Misery had gone. Not only had the chain broken again, but the frame welding had broken as well. This time with no money, no extra links or rivets and no ideas left to fix it, no one had to tell anyone that the bike was through.

Peter pulled his neck in and let his eyes circle the group. "We're close," he said. No one answered him. "Leave me here now. Morelli can meet me. He certainly isn't going to count my staying behind against our team."

Jerry stood up and taking his rag, wiped down the battered Raleigh. Peter looked away from him to Thad and Chris. "It's the only right decision. You know I'm right."

Thad got off his bike and started to lock it. "Well, then, I stay, too," he said simply.

"Oh, great," Partini sighed. "Martyrs, martyrs everywhere and not an ounce to think."

Silence again. Jerry found himself rubbing at a mud spot probably hardened on the Raleigh for years. Then he suddenly sat by the side of the bike. Across the woods he could see an island in the river with trees bent the way of the hurricane, driftwood and branches dried right up against the trees and rocks as if stopped in action. He felt tired. It would have felt good to have been out on the rocks sunning. Maybe to have Mimi braiding his hair. Or watching Peter and Thad discussing the turtle and the way its tail curled under the shell. He felt as if things were falling apart. After finally getting it together it was falling apart. Maybe a hero would have helped.

But Peter was right. They had to leave him behind. There was nothing else to do. If they had money they could rent a bike at Swain's Basin just ahead. If they had tools, they could fix the bike. But the truth was, they had nothing. They didn't even have a real night's food: the coconut shavings and raisins. All they had was each other, and, joke or no joke, that wasn't going to make it.

Thad hung his head, a flat expression crossing his face. "I'm staying."

Jerry walked over to him. "Look, Thad, at a certain point, we have to think about what we're trying to do . . . what Morelli's game is all about. Don't we?"

Thad shrugged.

"Well?" Jerry urged him.

"Sure." He seemed to understand, but then added, "But I'm not going without Peter."

Partini hit the top of his head with his palm. "You're supposed to be the big wizard. Did you ever hear of a wizard who quit?"

Thad sucked in the sides of his cheeks. "No," he said, his eyes fastened on Partini.

"Well . . . then?"

"I'm not quitting, I'm just not going . . ."

Chris was building a small fire in a tepee of sticks, neatly placing branch after branch in the pyramid. Jerry lay back on his sleeping bag, completely frustrated, and watched Thad take out a miniature chess set which he set between himself and Peter.

"Thad," Peter started as if he were going to convince him along with the others, but Thad shook his head stubbornly.

As if absolutely disgusted with the whole scene, Partini changed into a clean pair of skivvies and a clean tee shirt which blared in silver: RIDE THE WIND, BABY, and climbed into his sleeping bag. Chris, finally satisfied with his fire, started to hum.

"Words, Bard," Jerry prompted.

Chris grinned. "Hmmmmmmm. *Tell us where the dragons are . . . um . . . and we will all defeat them, we have tall and we have short . . . and,"* he looked up at Jerry, *"we have fire to beat them."*

"Lord, Chris. Hum!" Partini shouted from his sleeping bag.

But Chris went on. *"Canal streams, fire beams, strings that string of road beams, give us clues, any kind . . . we have fire to beat them."*

Partini sat up. "Your songs are really bad, Chris. No, has anyone ever told you that? I'm serious. You have a nice touch, if you had a guitar—or whatever that is—that didn't sound like the back of an upright piano—but you ought never to sing. Keep humming, like this," he pursed his lips at Chris, "H-mmmmmm-mmmmmmmmmmmm."

Chris shook his head and went on strumming while Jerry turned over and watched Gollum and the Wizard huddled over the chess board.

But that night Jerry couldn't go to sleep. The crickets were noisy in the woods behind them. A faint smell of trashcan that hadn't been collected kept blowing past him. He had been with Partini too long to ignore it. At one point, he even heard voices, a faraway laugh, floating from a farmhouse across the field. It was the first time he had heard voices at night. They really were getting close.

It was time to think about getting to Washington. It would be good to beat out Bull Templeton and his jocks. Maybe Bull's cocky expression would disappear for a minute anyway, but beat the others or not, what they were there for, the four of them, was to get to Washington. That's what Morelli really wanted. The ring, of course, was stupid. What Morelli said first was, get there. That was Morelli's game. Jerry turned over and stared down the dark and empty towpath; it really did look like a tunnel at night. His ideas sounded tinny. Like what? Like the coach at the junior high who said: "Look, the point of the game is to win." Damn, that ring bugged him. Why did Morelli mention it if it weren't important at all?

Suddenly, Chris whispered across at him. Jerry hadn't even known he was awake. "Remember the day Morelli talked about rings?" Chris said.

Jerry turned on his stomach and looked at Chris

lying crossways ten feet away. The hobbit had been after a ring; that's all Jerry remembered.

Chris went on, "He said the ring messes up a lot of people . . . and things."

"Whatever the hell that means," Jerry said.

Chris started to hum.

"I still prefer words."

Chris grinned.

"Maybe," Chris started to whisper louder, "maybe it doesn't matter what the ring is; the ring is whatever is at the end of the journey."

Jerry stared at him, then rolled over on his back. "Washington," he said, "but if a person lets the ring go to his head . . . I mean, if we let getting to Washington go to our heads . . . toss out something—or someone—that matters . . . we've let the ring . . ."

". . . mess us up," Chris filled in.

Jerry rubbed his throbbing jaw—another bruise that would turn blue tomorrow—but then he settled back. One cricket had obviously crawled into the vicinity of his bag. He listened to it closely, and to Partini who was scavenging in the bottom of his sleeping bag for something.

"Chris," Jerry whispered. "I vote Gollum goes with us."

"Two," Chris said.

Partini straightened his bag. "All right, three."

Jerry looked over at the contented mountain and the stringy sidekick who slept next to him. The plastic-wrapped chess set still lay between them—stalemated—but all Jerry heard was the whistling of air as Peter's tremendous cheeks blew in and out.

Jerry turned over in his sleeping bag when he heard Partini crawl over next to his ear.

"And Jerry?"

"Hmmmm?"

"I found something in my sleeping bag."

"A cricket," Jerry said.

"No . . . you don't understand . . . I had a ridiculously short time to pack this morning."

"Yes, Partini, yes."

"The lunches. I found the lunches in my sleeping bag."

Jerry got up on his elbows and started to laugh. "Poor conductor. He didn't steal anything. You bugger, Partini!"

Partini crawled back to his bag, silently.

"Forget it, Partini. It's a great relief to find out you're not perfect."

29

At dawn Jerry's stomach growled hungrily as if the
sides were grinding against each other. Never in his
life had he been so hungry, but they'd save Partini's
miracle lunch for the last push. He got up and moved
quickly among the sleeping bags spread around the
campsite like someone's thrown away rags.

"Let's go, Partini. No shaving. Chris, pack the mandolin; we're moving. Thad, you ride first. Take us there,
buddy." Jerry moved over to Peter, a giant sleeping in
his tossed-over bag, still on his back, still blowing his
cheeks in and out with each new breath.

"Come on, Pete," he said. "We're moving out."
Peter raised himself on his elbows, puzzled, as packs
were rolled and tied on the bikes, his turtle crawling up
and down the folds of his sleeping bag.

"Get with it, Pete."

"But I'm not going."

Jerry took the handlebars of Peter's Raleigh, dragged it off the path into the thick brush and left it hidden there, while Peter gaped at him.

Then Jerry turned. "You're riding my bike, Pete. I'll ride rumble seat. You've got five minutes."

"I don't think . . ." Peter started.

"We didn't ask you to," Partini said. "We know that's difficult."

Zap.

Pete grinned and shook his head. "You're all mad!" he said.

"You must know my father," Jerry said over his shoulder. "That's what he says." And he tied Peter's pack onto Thad's bike.

Partini skipped the deodorant spray and sped out first, still clothed in his shirt and pants from the night before, and his original orange flowered headband. His one boot was as caked with mud as his baggy pants. Thad went second with Peter and Jerry close behind him until Jerry called ahead: "Take it out, Thad," and Thad pedaled to the front of the line.

"Go," he shouted back.

Full to brimming, the canal was covered with water lilies, and turtles dozed on sun-baked logs, slipping off as the unexpected bikes raced past them. Jerry began to smell Washington. Not in so many fumes, not as he smelled New York when he reached the George Washington Bridge. But there was something in the air.

Peter hulked in front of Jerry bearing down huskily on each push, not quick and wiry like Jerry, more like a great bear. By the time they reached Swain's Canal,

173

Lock 21, the owners were just pushing up the pine-slated windows and pulling out the what-is-there-to-eat sign. The smell of day-old hamburger grease was thick. It almost drove Jerry mad. Peter gave out a huge sigh, but the time wasn't right to stop yet.

Thad didn't slow down anyway.

"I'm starving!" Partini wailed.

Chris took over for Peter just past Swain's, with Jerry still hugging the rear. That was a change. Chris's thin shoulders worked twice as fast as Peter's and his feet seemed barely to touch the pedals, almost as if he were running on his toes over frost.

As the river widened, more and more people strode down the towpath, forcing the four bikes to weave in and out to avoid them. Then, suddenly, through the tunnel, a grass-green lawn spread out toward a terrace of concrete buildings.

"Great Falls Park," Chris announced as they passed a sign saying the same thing.

"Thanks," Jerry said. On trips his mother was a sign reader, too.

At 10:30 in the morning, the place already teemed with people. Cars of assorted colors and brilliance jockeyed for spaces. People surrounding a gray-haired older woman crowded together for a picture on a concrete apron that overlooked the river. There wasn't a sign of a crazy towpath here. No dragons. No Mirkwood. No slime. Even the locks had turned tame, doors hooked back neatly, new flowers planted around their edge. Thad stubbornly sped right by.

"Smell it?" Jerry grinned around Chris. "W-A-S-H-I-N-G-T-O-N."

"And the ring!" Chris said.

"Ring nothing. I want a pizza, with an extra order of cheese and mushrooms."

A park attendant stopped sweeping to glare at them.

"With anchovies," Chris added.

Outside the park Jerry and Chris switched, an even better combination. Peter went on clunking along. With Chris's paraphernalia and his turtle bag on top, he looked like the neighborhood rag man at the end of a big day.

The towpath grew tamer. No brawling canal captains or Roman aqueducts, no mile-long rock paths. Signs to the Great Falls almost caught them.

"Let's stop," Partini shouted, "I'm beginning to perspire!"

"No way, Ho-zay," Thad called back. He never lifted his head. He was all go.

When an empty lake they were passing narrowed into a gravel pass between two hills, they looked up to see ahead of them a concrete wall of some sort built right across the towpath. It had to be eighteen feet high.

"Morelli did it again!" Partini announced.

It was true. The structure made no sense at all. It was as if a game board read: *Impassable wall.* Return to Go, do not collect two hundred dollars. But that didn't slow Thad either. He rode dead ahead. At the structure, he climbed off and swept his bike into his hands. He called Partini to help him and the two of them started up the rain-washed path, an almost perpendicular rock path at the side of the wall. No one spoke; they just hustled to follow Thad. By the time

175

Peter stopped his bike, Thad and Partini had lifted
Thad's bike over the top. Partini didn't even give a
monologue on sweat.

Jerry flipped off his bike, and along with Peter,
grabbed Chris's bike, and they started up the path,
too, looking for footholds as they climbed. Suddenly,
the packs fell upside down and the mandolin fell out of
the loose ropes. It bounced off the back of the seat,
against the wall, and down the rocks, neck over bottom over neck. Eighteen feet. Jerry followed it, taking
the hill in jumps, and just before it hit the ground, he
threw his hand under it.

Chris sat down and stared at the ridiculous brown
bowl of an instrument.

"No problem," Jerry said and handed it to him.

"Hustle!" Thad called.

The other two bikes were quickly manhandled up
the hill.

Before they could start off again, however, they
realized Peter had slipped away to a small pond in the
woods nearby. Still carrying his bag, Peter, sneakers
on, was sloshing into a mucky shallow toward a tiny
moss-covered peninsula.

"Hustle, Pete!" Thad called again.

But now Peter refused. He reached into his bag,
gently took out the brown turtle and set it on the finger
of land. The turtle sat for a minute, like one more
clump of moss, tail, legs and head tucked into its shell,
then slowly, the head poked out and the turtle stretched
its neck and blinked.

"Now I'm ready," Peter said.

That was the last bit of the wild world. Shortly after,

Jerry could hear the silent hum of cars, and then he saw ahead of them the hulking feet of a super highway stalking over the path. The towpath almost seemed to be gasping for breath as it passed a series of locks: fourteen, thirteen, twelve, eleven.

"In case I forgot to tell you, Sebastian," Partini shouted at the last lock, "I won't miss your sneakers."

It was clear now: the scene was Washington. A street flew over the towpath on a bridge. On their left, neat brick colonial houses pressed closer and closer, their wavy old glass windows overflowing with spring flowers, until there were only the houses, towpath and the canal racing neck and neck toward Washington.

Ahead, Jerry could see another street, this one running right across the towpath. Stupid street! Jerry wanted to shout at it. What right had anyone to let cars pour across the towpath? It had tunneled itself past washed-out bridges and crumbling aqueducts and eighteen-foot walls.

But as they rolled up the hill toward the busy street, Thad still didn't slow down. A Volkswagen screeched to a stop as Thad pedaled right across the line of traffic, ignoring it completely, and Peter rolled after him.

"We've neither brain nor sinew . . ." Chris wailed as Jerry followed them without a break, and Partini made it a string. Cars honked furiously at the bikers, but they stayed hunched together staring straight down the towpath, stopping for no one—not cars, not trucks, not pedestrians. They had earned right of way.

When they got to Memorial Bridge, the city struck and suddenly the towpath simply disappeared in a maze of boulevards. Amid fumes, screeching brakes, honking horns, the cars whizzed around the circular sweeping bridge. Jerry wondered what Thad was hesitating for, when Thad suddenly made a sweep around the other bikes to the rear and Peter did the same, and Jerry realized everyone was behind him.

It was for him to take them into the center.

He didn't even feel the weight of Chris, as he coasted down the scooped curb into the city. It was wilderness of a new kind. Streets that ran in one-way circles. Sidewalks set in mazes that led to giant white buildings. The Jefferson Memorial . . . Lincoln Memorial.

Jerry felt something all right. It wasn't the pizza though. He had even forgotten about Partini's lunch. It wasn't Bull either. It was something else. Something inside Jerry. Something for Morelli, and, yes, Lockewood. Maybe Partini was right. There would be other dragons, other tunnels, but they had gotten through this one, and when he saw the Washington Monument from the top of the concrete apron, he whooped down the hill into the path that ran along the pond. Nothing could stop them now.

Chris's legs stuck straight out like wings on a jet, as they coasted down the hill, and Thad sang out a "Whoooop," as his bike flew down the pathway after them.

"There it is," Peter panted evenly, still chugging, bringing up the rear.

Chris started to hum as Jerry hit the end of the strip with the Monument streaking up into the sky on the hill ahead of them, just a hum, but then he started singing at the top of his voice.

"You can take your dragons, your dungeons and your slime and push them in a stairway to the sky . . ."

"You really shouldn't sing, Chris," Partini shouted.

Jerry grinned as he pedaled into the street toward the hostelry. He had two thoughts. Too bad Mimi couldn't be with them now, and he had never seen Partini so rumpled in his life.

ABOUT THE AUTHOR

PATRICIA LEE GAUCH grew up in Michigan and was educated at Miami University in Ohio and Manhattanville College in New York, and did graduate work in English at Drew University.

After graduating from Miami, Ms. Gauch worked as a newspaper journalist for several years before turning to children's fiction. She writes eight months of the year and spends the rest of her time teaching high school. She enjoys the interaction with young adults and has gotten many ideas for her books from them. *Morelli's Game* was inspired by many classroom discussions and a bike trip she took with a youth group. The author has tried to portray the unpredictability of life, and the subsequent risks we must take in our wanderings, with a group of characters every young person will recognize.

Ms. Gauch enjoys traveling abroad but makes her home in Basking Ridge, New Jersey, with her husband and three children.